MARTIN'S COTTAGE

MARTIN'S COTTAGE

*A Novella of Cornwall
and Other Stories*

DENYS VAL BAKER

WILLIAM KIMBER · LONDON

First published in 1983 by
WILLIAM KIMBER & CO. LIMITED
100 Jermyn Street,
London SW1Y 6EE

ISBN 0-7183-0379-2

Photoset in North Wales by
Derek Doyle & Associates, Mold, Clwyd
and printed in Great Britain by
Biddles Limited, Guildford.

Contents

I

Martin's Cottage

1

When Richard Eames came upon Martin's Cottage he thought it was one of the most romantic places he had ever seen. Set high up on the cliffs not far from Land's End, it was one of the old Cornish granite cottages that seem to grow out of the surrounding grassy slopes. Inside the place had been modernised but the long, low cross-beams remained and it was possible to see the immense thickness of the walls, indented along one side by a great open fireplace with blue-slated seats. The walls were white-washed so that everywhere seemed bright and gay with not a hint of the darkness which had once shrouded the building (though this he did not even suspect). Above all else the cottage possessed a unique and magical view, the big bow window of the sitting room looking directly out upon the surging Atlantic waves, with the stark outline of the Longships lighthouse rearing up in the distance.

Richard fell in love with the place at once and as soon as he got back to Penzance walked into the estate agent's office and made an offer there and then. To his delight this was accepted, and after a few impatient weeks while the legal side was sorted out finally, one glorious September day they moved out there – himself and his wife Nora and their seventeen-year-old daughter Karen, together with a lorry-load of possessions and furnishings.

At first the three of them seemed busy all the time laying carpets and moving furniture and establishing each room's identity – the small loft bedroom for Karen, the larger one below for Nora and Richard, the big long sitting-room for communal purposes, the small alcove at one side (also with a breathtaking view) making an ideal spot for a writer to work away vigorously. Then gradually, as first the weeks and then the months slipped by, Richard found that at last it was possible to relax a little, to savour more fully the marvels of living in such a hauntingly beautiful spot.

At least, that was how it seemed to him. Sadly he began to see that Nora did not altogether share his enthusiasm. One morning he looked up and saw her standing accusingly in the kitchen doorway.

'That wind! Do you know it's never stopped blowing since the day we moved in?'

'We *are* at the end of the land.'

'The end of the land indeed. I've never seen anywhere quite so bleak. When I come down in the mornings and open the front door I look out on just one vast expanse of hostile sea. I could be living on an island. It's the same if I go out. There's just the cliffs and treeless fields stretching everywhere, solitary rocks and even more solitary clumps of scattered cottages ...'

'You must admit the place certainly has atmosphere. And what a strange history! Why, only the other day that old fisherman down in the cove was telling me all about Martin, the way he built the place with his own two hands – *the whole place*. It took two years – two whole years.' Richard shook his head wonderingly. 'What intrigues me is – why has it always remained Martin's Cottage? Once or twice apparently people have tried to give it more fancy names, Cove Cottage, Sea View, that sort of thing; but they never caught on. In the end it's always the same – Martin's Cottage.'

Nora shrugged.

'Well, anyway, I must get on with lunch. Where's Karen?'

'I don't know – she went out some time ago.'

'I do wish she'd say whether she'd be in for lunch. Just because we're living in the wilds she seems to think she can come and go as she pleases.'

Richard opened his mouth to reply and then closed it again. There was no point in resuming the eternal argument about their strange and somewhat fey daughter. At this stage in her life he felt she should be free like the wind itself whereas Nora was always on to her to get a job and settle down and that sort of thing. Perhaps not surprisingly Karen seemed closer to himself than to her mother, and even less surprisingly this rankled.

A little later, looking out of the window, he saw Karen coming up the steps. Wearing the singlet and jeans that seemed to be almost the regular uniform of the young she looked nevertheless very much at home in the windswept surroundings, her long dark hair blowing back in the breeze, her eyes bright with inner excitement. When she came in he could not resist calling out:

'Feeling happy?'

'Oh, yes! I've been along the cliffs. There are masses of violets and sea pinks – they grow in the most incredible places, in between rocks and everywhere. Alan's been explaining all about them.'

'Alan?'

'One of the lighthousekeepers. He was out on the cliffs and we got talking. He's nice.'

Richard hesitated but decided not to labour the point. A few minutes later Nora called them for lunch. It was a simple meal of salad and cheese which should have passed pleasantly enough but somehow Nora and Richard started arguing, pettily but persistently, so that in the end Karen interrupted, demanding to know why Nora spoke so bitterly. What had Richard done wrong?

'It's what he *hasn't* done. It's not easy week after week wondering where the money is going to come from, listening all the time to the tapping of a typewriter and knowing that all it's doing is pinning down passing thoughts and fancies. Do you realise it's months since your father earned any money?'

She began clearing away noisily, obviously upset, but not yet finished with what she wanted to say.

'And anyway this place – well there's a strange feeling about it. Haven't you noticed?'

'What sort of feeling?'

'I don't know how to put it. A sensation of being hemmed in, as if the walls are closing in on me. It's stupid, I suppose, but sometimes I get the impression I'm in a prison and I have a terrible desire to escape.'

When Nora had gone to the kitchen Karen got up and went over to the window, staring out. Looking at her Richard felt a pang of affection. What a strange creature she was – and yet, instinctively, he felt he understood even her confusion.

'I feel quite the opposite,' she said. 'I've never been so happy as since I came here. Mind you, I must admit there's something curiously *familiar* about it all. When I was walking back this morning I felt glad to be coming back to this cottage, Martin's Cottage. I felt safer, I tried to explain it to Alan ...'

As Karen finished speaking, Nora came back into the room.

'What's this Alan like?'

'Oh, nice. Quiet.'

'How did you meet him?'

'On the cliffs, watching the seagulls.'

'Haven't you anything better to do than watch the seagulls and talk to lighthousekeepers?'

Karen flushed.

'I can't think of a nicer way to spend my life.'

'There are so many other things, Karen. The world's a big place.' Nora looked around her with sudden distaste. 'Much bigger than Martin's Cottage.'

'Perhaps you're right, Mother. All the same I'll swop your big world for this little one.' Karen pushed away the plate and jumped to her feet. 'Anyway, I think I'll go out again ... it's such a beautiful day.'

When she had gone Nora looked at Richard in exasperation but said nothing. She picked up a magazine and went and curled up by the window and began reading. Watching her he was aware uneasily of a growing distance between them – but pushed away the unwelcome thought.

Left to his own resources Richard allowed his mind to start

wandering. He thought about all the people that must have occupied Martin's Cottage in the past. The room he was sitting in was where children had played, where old people sat dying in – above all this was the room that once upon a time Martin built with his own hands. That was what so fascinated him, had done ever since he saw the house. He couldn't help feeling there was some sort of eternal challenge.

He wasn't thinking just about the elements either. He was thinking about something else that the old fisherman had told him. The fact that although several families had lived here since Martin's time none of them had stayed more than a year or two. He felt curious about the reasons – what were the impulses that had led them to move again? He wished he could have talked to some of the people but now there seemed no way of tracing them. Perhaps he would never know the answer.

Richard shook his head firmly. No, that needn't be the end of the matter. After all, Martin's Cottage was his now – if anyone could uncover its secrets then surely it was himself.

He leaned back and looked around the already familiar room. There must be *some* way of unravelling its secret.

Just at that moment Nora turned from the window warningly.

'Someone's coming up the steps ...'

2

For the next half hour Richard and Nora occupied the two armchairs, while on the sofa in the middle of the room sat their visitor, a large powerfully built, thick-set man, dark and rather forbidding-looking, dressed soberly in a dark suit and with a cloth cap on his lap.

'Well,' said Nora politely. 'You don't seem to have lost your Cornish accent, Mr Trewella, even after all your years of exile.'

''Spose not, ma'am. Once a Cornishman allus a Cornishman, they say.'

'That's true,' said Richard. 'I've never met a more clannish lot.'

' 'Tis right, mister. They do keep to thessels a good deal. 'Spect you've found that out?'

Nora smiled.

'They may keep to themselves but they've still got a healthy interest in everyone else's affairs.'

Richard looked at her caustically.

'What do *you* know of the Cornish?'

'More than you, burying yourself up here. I'm always chatting to the people in the village ... Mrs Hosking and Mrs George and that old man who paces up and down the cliffs waiting to lure visitors into letting him be their guide.'

The swarthy man on the couch showed a flash of emotion.

'Ole Billy Stevens? A proper windbag, Billy Stevens! And Nancy George? Does she still keep the village shop?'

'Yes. You remember her?'

'Aye. A lot more besides.'

Richard stirred.

'How long since you went away?'

'Fifteen years or more.'

'And you've never been back?'

The big Cornishman shook his head.

'Packed my bag and caught the bus to Penzance and a train all the way to the docks at Southampton and that was the last time my feet touched British soil until the other day. Made meself a new life in South Africa.'

'That's where a lot of Cornish folk go, isn't it?'

''Tis right, yes. Miners mostly. You've maybe heard the saying, wherever there's a 'ole, like as not you'll find a Cornishman at the bottom. Plenty o' mines in South Africa.' Trewella shook his head thoughtfully. 'Very different to Cornwall, of course.'

'And now you've come back to settle?'

'Oh, no. I ain't come back at all, if you follows me. I jess caught the bus from Penzance out to Land's End, it being such a fine day like, and well I couldn't resist taking a bit of a walk along the cliffs. I weren't going to go down to the cove, not really, and then I sees the roof of Martin's Cottage and I thinks to meself, well, I'll just take a peep. I was going to take a look round for ole times' sake, so to speak. I allus sposed 'twould be empty, you see, didn't have no idea it would be occupied. 'Twas quite a shock to find someone answering the door.'

Richard looked at him curiously.

'Why did you knock, Mr Trewella, if you thought the place was empty?'

'Oh, I dunno, I jess knocked. Happen I thought ... at the last moment like ...'

'Did you think perhaps Martin would still be here?'

'No, no – niver. Martin's been dead these many years.'

Richard leaned forward excitedly.

'You knew him then? The Martin that built this cottage? Tell us about him. The name of the cottage – it's a constant reminder.'

Trewella looked thoughtful.

'You ain't changed the name then?' He hesitated, and then went on: 'Course I knew Martin. We were at school together – you know, the village school up the hill. We used to walk up every day, me and Martin and Harry George from the pub. Seems a long time ago now. Later on, when we'd growed up, we used to go fishin' together, night after night. We'd come back near dawn with our pots full, singing at the top of our voices. 'Twas a good life ...'

Trewella paused. He was about to speak again when he seemed to hear something. Quickly he got up and went to the window, looking agitated.

'There's some folk comin'. I'd rather net meet anyone. 'Twould be better not. I wan't meanin' to come back, you see.'

'You can go into the kitchen,' Nora said. 'You'll be quite all right there.'

'Thank'ee, ma'am, if you don't mind 'spect I can slip away round the back.'

Richard shook his head vehemently.

'Don't do that. There's a lot of things I want to ask you.'

With a nod that remained ambiguous, Trewella went across

the room and out into the kitchen, shutting the door behind him silently.

'Well,' said Nora, 'I wonder who –'

She went out into the hall just in time to respond to a ring on the bell by opening the front door. A few moments later she ushered into the sitting room two people – one a small bouncy man wearing the obvious clerical uniform of the local vicar, the other a more dominating individual dressed more smartly in town clothes; a man in his late forties grey-haired, keen-faced and exuding a sense of confidence and power.

'How do you do?' said the clerical gentleman. 'My name is Robert Lanyon, from the vicarage down in the village. I called once before but you must have been out. I didn't leave my card – we vicars don't go in for them much now, though I sometimes think it might be a good idea in these scattered country districts. So many journeys to be made, often to no purpose ... Anyway, may I introduce Mr Bruce – Mr Arnold Bruce?'

Richard and Nora nodded politely to the other stranger.

'Down for a visit, Mr Bruce?' said Richard.

'Yes, I own some property in the district so I like to keep an eye on things. But I live in London normally – near Green Park.'

'I remember taking walks there,' said Nora, speaking with sudden animation. 'London parks can be so lovely.'

Bruce looked at her curiously.

'London has much to be said for it.'

'And Cornwall?'

'Cornwall can be a gold mine – with the right handling.'

Nora laughed.

'Is that what you supply, Mr Bruce? The right handling?'

'I think so. I've made quite a lot of money out of Cornwall already. I intend to make a lot more.'

'An admirable ambition, Mr Bruce,' said Richard blandly. 'And one that I'm sure will appeal to my wife.'

'It certainly does,' said Nora quickly. 'It's all very well for writers and artists to talk about money as if it were mud.'

'Money has its uses,' said Bruce mildly.

'Ah, yes,' said Richard. 'But money can't buy love. It can't build friendship. It can't create great art.'

Bruce shrugged.

'All the same people are foolish when they run away from the idea of money. It's powerful. Very often it enables one to get ... what one wants.'

In the pause that followed Richard turned to the little vicar.

'I was wondering, Mr Lanyon, if you've been in the parish a long time whether you ever knew our predecessor here? I mean, of course, the man who built his place?'

'I knew him a little. However I only came here a few months before his, er ...'

'His death?'

'His, er, *presumed* death. The body was never actually found.'

'Really,' said Richard. 'It all sounds very mysterious.'

Opposite him Bruce stirred impatiently.

'Come, there's enough romantic nonsense talked about Cornwall as it is without building up a little myth of your own. What happened to the fellow then that his death couldn't be proved?'

'He disappeared quite suddenly,' said the vicar. 'Later his boat was found drifting. I imagine they took it for granted he had fallen overboard and been drowned. But no one actually saw him going to sea and the body was never found.'

'I thought there was a saying that the sea always yielded up its dead,' said Nora.

'Oh no, Mrs Eames, that isn't strictly true. Sometimes they just disappear into the deep and are never seen again. Martin was one of those.'

Richard held up an admonishing finger.

'You mean Martin *might* have been one of those?'

The vicar nodded.

'Tell me,' went on Richard. 'What else did you learn about Martin? Was he married?'

'No, but apparently there was a girl, once ... In general he seems to have been rather a solitary man. He lived here for many years quite alone. But at one time there was this girl. It

was before my time but apparently he was very devoted to her
... unfortunately she died. I never quite understood the
circumstances except that she was drowned.'

'Like Martin?'

'Well, not quite. *Her* body was found ... washed up on the
sands.'

Nora grimaced.

'How horrible. What a shock for poor Martin.'

'Yes, I gather it quite unbalanced him. When they came
and told him he just refused to believe them.'

Bruce moved impatiently.

'But the body – surely that convinced him?'

'Not at all – for the very good reason that he never saw it.
He just shut himself up in the cottage for days on end ... in
other words, he shut the girl's death out of his comprehension.
To him it was as if she never drowned, she never died – though
in fact you can see her gravestone in my churchyard. No, from
that day on Martin became a recluse, a hermit, cutting
himself off from the life of the village. The only time he
appeared was to go out in his boat – even then the villagers say
he never took any nets with him. They say – I suppose it's
become a bit of a legend now – they say he just went searching
for his girl. Apparently he swore that one day he would find
her and bring her home!' He shrugged. 'I mean of course –
here, to Martin's Cottage.'

Richard would like to have pursued his inquiries but
suddenly the Reverend Lanyon said he had to be going.
However he would leave Mr Bruce as the latter had a matter
he wished to discuss with Richard.

When the vicar had gone Richard looked inquiringly in the
direction of their other visitor.

'The fact is,' said Bruce, 'I have a project on, quite a big
one.'

'Man of action, eh?'

'You can be sarcastic. But I'll be blunt with you I'd rather
be in my shoes with all that I am and own today than I would
be in yours stuck in this little cottage on the edge of nowhere.'

'Don't you think there are many people who might envy us?

A writer is free – free to roam the world, to live where he likes – to live how he likes.'

'But Richard,' Nora interrupted impatiently. 'Without money we're even more tied than Mr Bruce, who I gather is rolling in gold.'

Bruce sighed.

'Not exactly, Mrs Eames. I am a man of means, granted. Mind you, I've got ambitions, too, a man must have a purpose in life.'

'Agreed, Mr Bruce,' said Richard. 'You have your purpose, I have mine. What could be fairer?'

'Quite. Unfortunately sometimes the purposes conflict.' He cleared his throat. 'As you know, Cornwall does have a magical sort of quality that you can't find anywhere else in Britain. Well, for a long time I've planned to capitalise upon that attraction. I'm convinced that given the right sort of background and facilities one can create holiday centres in Cornwall that will outrival anything the French Riviera or anywhere else can offer. But it is no good doing things in a fiddly way, one's got to think *big*. And – well, that brings me to the project I'm talking about. I've raised all the capital and it's going ahead.'

'What is it?' said Nora with obvious interest. 'Do tell us.'

'It's right here, Mrs Eames. I'm going to make this isolated little fishing village into one of the centres of the Cornish Riviera. Can you imagine it? Why it's got everything you could want from the natural point of view – tropical weather, wonderful bay, beautiful sands, glorious cliffs. All that's needed is the proper accommodation. That's where I come in. We're going to build a complete holiday centre as luxurious as any you could find. Hot and cold showers, fully equipped restaurants, lounges, playrooms, dormitories, discos ...'

'How perfectly ghastly!' exclaimed Richard.

'What's ghastly about it? You must realise that nowadays people want comfort and good service with their holidays. The time's gone when they'll put up with sour-faced landladies and petty rules and regulations.'

Nora leaned forward.

'It's certainly quite exciting. I mean to plan it all out and have a whole project, then to see it come to reality.'

'Oh, it's all come to reality all right. We've already purchased nearly all the property. I'm down now just to tie up the loose ends.'

'I still don't understand,' said Richard. 'How does it affect us?'

'It's quite simple really. The site for our centre will extend over a large area. At one end it will finish by the harbour. At the other end the boundary will be the coastguard hut. In depth it will stretch back as far as the top road. Everything in that area will be incorporated into my complex.'

'You mean ...?'

'Naturally we shall want to purchase Martin's Cottage. It stands almost in the middle of things. We're prepared to offer a very fair price, of course. Something in the region of forty or fifty thousand. It's worth it to complete our plans.'

'Fifty thousand pounds!' Nora looked startled. She turned. 'That's a lot of money, Richard.'

Richard made an impatient gesture.

'Fifty thousand pounds – all that and then I suppose you'd raze the place to the ground?'

'I'm not sure. It's a fine old Cornish cottage – we might leave it as it is, make it a sort of show-place. Perhaps still call it Martin's Cottage – you know, play up the haunted side. I mean we might conjure up some legend of a ghost, something like that.'

'A ghost? My God, yes, I wonder what Martin would have thought of it all? I wonder if the man who spent two years putting down the granite blocks and mixing cement, seeing each wall rise slowly to the sky – what he would think of a crowd of holidaymakers milling around here?'

Nora gave an exclamation.

'Oh, do let's forget Martin for once! I tell you, it's not healthy the way you keep thinking about him.'

Richard looked at her pointedly.

'It's all very well to say forget about Martin. This was *his* cottage, remember?'

'Well, all right, and now Mr Bruce is offering us fifty thousand pounds for it. Let him worry about Martin.' She looked at Richard pleadingly. 'Think of it, Richard – fifty thousand pounds. We could travel, buy new clothes, clear off our debts. It might make all the difference between –'

'Between what? You were going to say between success and failure, weren't you, Nora. That's because you're really just like Bruce here. You think of everything in material terms. Success is money, failure is lack of money.'

Bruce cleared his throat.

'Your wife is right, you know.'

Richard sighed.

'I expect so. But – I'm damned if I'm going to agree, Mr Bruce. Ever since I came into this cottage I've had a feeling upon me, a strange sort of feeling – a sense of responsibility if you like, of being impelled by some force, some purpose. I can't explain it, and I don't expect you to understand it. But now I think I'm beginning to understand better. If there's one thing I'd bet on, it's that if Martin were alive today he'd tell you to whistle for his cottage – yes, even if you were to offer a hundred thousand pounds. And that's my answer to you, Mr Bruce.'

In the long pause that ensued Richard began walking up and down the room as if to calm himself. Bruce looked from him to Nora, and then got to his feet.

'You're a bit overwrought now, Mr Eames, I think we'd better leave it for the moment. But there's my offer, fifty thousand pounds. I'll call back later when you've had time to think matters over.'

Nora rose.

'I'm sure Richard will change his mind on reflection. Here, I'll see you out.'

As they went towards the door Bruce said casually:

'It's a lovely afternoon, Mrs Eames. Would you care to come a little way with me?'

'Yes, Why not? A stroll will do me good.'

3

When the two of them had gone Richard moved restlessly about the room, clasping and unclasping his hands. Somehow, despite all his anger and bluster, he felt a little afraid. Men like Bruce were dangerous, they almost invariably got their way.

As he was still wandering around, lost in thought, the kitchen door opened and Trewella came in a little sheepishly.

· 'Good heavens, I'd forgotten – did you hear what was going on? That awful man wants to buy the cottage and make it part of some dreadful holiday complex.'

He made a beckoning gesture.

'Anyway, come and sit down, Mr Trewella. We were interrupted in the middle of an interesting conversation about Martin's Cottage. Did you hear what Mr Lanyon was saying? I'm particularly interested you see because – well because I'm a writer, and the whole subject fascinates me. Now look, Mr Lanyon says there was a girl – Martin's girl.'

To his surprise Trewella's reaction was an angry one.

'Doan't you listen to what that vicar man says. 'Ee doan't know nothing about it at all. Nobody knows nothin', do you understand? Nobody.'

'Only Martin, eh?'

'Maybe ...'

'And you?'

'Look, mister, I've told you. I've niver been near this place for nigh on fifteen years. I've been away all that time, thousands of miles away, in South Africa. I'd niver have come back if it 'adn't been for ...'

'For what?'

'I dunno. I – er, jess wanted to come back, that was the way of it.'

'Suddenly, just out of the blue? Surely you must often have thought about returning? Didn't you feel homesick?'

'Ah, well, mister, yes, a Cornishman is allus homesick.

Many's the night I've lain awake out there in the veldt not able to get off to sleep, staring up at the stars. You know, out there it's quite different somehow. I used to lie there wanting so much to smell the sea – it got a real passion with me, mister. One day, do you know, I travelled three hundred miles to the coast jess to see the sea. But it wasn't the same, somehow. There were miles of flat sands and the sea was dead calm.'

'Not like here, eh? Well, never mind all that. Tell me what *really* made you come home after all this time?'

Trewella hesitated and for a moment it seemed that he would dry up. In desperation Richard brought up again the question of the girl Martin had been involved with and suddenly, to his surprise, the other man began talking.

'She was called Davida. A pretty name ... She was a right pretty thing, too. Yes, you never saw anyone quite as pretty. She had long dark hair hanging over her shoulders; she would do it up in tresses like for Sunday school and that sort o' thing. I mind when she had pigtails, too, but that was before she was a woman. That was when she were still a girl at school.'

'Davida – was that a local name?'

'Well, it was like this. You see, her old man 'ee did really want a boy an' they were going to call him David. So when it was a girl – well I s'pose the old man was disappointed like and to make it seem less of a disappointment they kept the name.'

'I don't think I've come across the name before.'

'Tisn't likely, mister. Not many like that. No one like Davida.'

'Mr Lanyon was saying—— '

Trewella's face darkened.

'Niver mind what Mr Lanyon was saying. And doan't you ask me any more, mister. I'm telling you – you doan't have no right to be asking me questions about such things.'

'I'm sorry. Does it upset you?'

'It's being 'ere, in this place – it all brings back so much, you see.'

'I can imagine that.' Richard sighed. 'It's all very confusing.'

He turned and went across to the window, staring out.

'I'd best be on my way, mister.'

'No, stay a while. You can have some tea with us – my wife will be back soon, I expect.'

As he spoke Richard went on staring out of the window. Looking down the long winding steps, he could see Nora and Bruce nearing the end. They seemed to be engaged in animated conversation. Somehow the sight bothered him, and he turned away.

'Excuse me, will you? I'll just go in the kitchen and put a kettle on.'

As soon as Richard had gone out of the room Trewella seemed to become a man suddenly transformed with purpose. He crossed quickly to the fireplace and there turned and surveyed the room carefully. He began moving round the room slowly, every now and then touching the wall, a window, the door. About his actions there was a curious touch of emotion, of veneration, almost of love. Finally he came back to the centre of the room and sat down on the couch, lost in thought.

Suddenly from outside there came the sound of someone climbing up the steps ... A moment later the door swung open and Karen stood framed in the doorway. She had obviously continued her walk down to the beach and taken a quick swim, for her towel and bathing costume were under her arm, and she looked slightly dishevelled, her hair hanging in long damp tresses over her shoulders. She was about to come into the centre of the room when she saw the unfamiliar figure of Trewella, and gave a slight exclamation.

His reverie broken, Trewella gave a start and looked up. In an instant his whole figure was transfixed. He half rose to his feet, behaving like a man who had seen a ghost.

'Davida!' He choked, and then called out the name more loudly. 'Davida!'

Then as Richard came back in from the kitchen, with a gasping sound Trewella spun round and ran towards the doorway, disappearing through it and into the bright sunlight.

4

The next morning was the occasion for the weekly visit from Miss Nicholas, a plump Cornishwoman, an ex-secretary who did shorthand and whose typing was much better than Richard's so that it was worth him employing her for important manuscripts. As usual they settled at Richard's desk in the alcove and plunged straight into work, with Richard dictating.

' ... the cottage fits so closely into the cliff that it seems to be as much a part of it as the moss-covered rocks that lunge up here and there like – like murmurs of the past. This encourages a false sense of security, a protection against the outside world ...'

He paused.

'A false sense of security – yes, I like that. Have you got that, Miss Nicholas? Good. Oh, by the way do you detect anything different in the atmosphere of this room?'

Miss Nicholas looked around rather uneasily, shaking her head.

'I just wondered. It was the scene of several surprising incidents yesterday. First, a man came here all the way from South Africa. Then another man called wanting to buy the cottage and my wife got angry because I wouldn't sell. Finally, my daughter was mistaken for a girl who died more than fifteen years ago. Quite a lot to happen in one day, don't you think?'

Richard stared rather accusingly at Miss Nicholas.

'I'm surprised you don't notice anything. To my mind this whole room is absolutely alive with strangeness, a feeling of mystery. Even my wife who's not normally particularly sensitive, even she feels it. By the way, did you see my wife down in the village?'

'Yes. She was in Mr Bruce's car – the big green one.'

'Oh, yes, I'd forgotten. He promised to take her for a drive. Funny man – so wrapped up in material possessions. It's rather ludicrous him wanting to buy Martin's Cottage, don't you think?'

Miss Nicholas looked embarrassed.

'Depends what he offers, I s'pose. I mean – I can remember the time when nobody would dream of buying the place, nobody niver came near.'

Nodding Richard stared up at the ceiling, endeavouring to gather his thoughts together. Unfortunately his attention was deviated by what he saw.

'Tell me, what are those curious lines marked out on the ceiling there?'

Miss Nicholas looked up.

'Why them's the mark of one of these old trap doors that used to be there. I spose you know about them? They were put there so that folk could slide down the coffins. Coffin hatches, my ole dad used to call them. You see, the stairs in these old cottages – they're so narrow and twisty, and most of them fishermen are great hefty fellows.'

'Mmmh. Funny to think that once Martin ...'

Miss Nicholas shook her head firmly.

'No, not Martin – 'ee was drowned at sea, or so they say.' She hesitated. 'Mind, some do say that his spirit still belongs to this cottage.'

'I can quite believe it. I don't mind telling you, Miss Nicholas, I have the feeling there's quite a story lurking between these four walls. My wife thinks it's all becoming a sort of obsession with me ... I must say I do feel some sort of compulsion to try and get at the truth.

'The truth?' Miss Nicholas shrugged decisively. 'Who's to know what's the truth in these matters?'

'Yes, well, we really must try and get on.' Richard gave an exclamation. 'Damn, I've lost it now! It's so difficult to concentrate. It's no good, we'll have to leave it for now. You'd better go home. I tell you what, it's a lovely day, I'll walk down with you. We might meet my wife coming back.'

Soon after they had gone out a shadow appeared at the top of the stairs and Karen came slowly down. She went over to her father's desk and looked curiously at some of the typed sheets, reading out aloud:

'From my window I have the impression of looking out upon not one but several different worlds. I sometimes wonder whether if each one of us were to think about it we would find that each of our windows offers a view of many worlds. I cannot believe –'

She stopped at the sound of a faint tap at the door. Crossing over, she opened it and Trewella came in, swiftly closing the door behind him.

'Look, girl, I'm sorry about the other day. I didn't mean to frighten you. All the same, it's damn strange ... damn strange indeed. The likeness ...' He passed a hand over his eyes as if to shield himself from the thought. 'The same age. The same way of looking. The same long hair. I tell you, it was almost too much for me to look at.'

Agitated, he began pacing up and down the room. After some hesitation Karen went and sat in one of the armchairs.

'I didn't say anything the other night,' she said, 'but I did have a strange feeling as if – as if we've met before. As a matter of fact when I was on the cliffs the other day I saw you in the distance and even then your walk had something about it – well, *familiar.* And then when you called out that name the other day something happened that really frightened me.'

'What was that?'

'It was as if you were crying – to *me*, not to Davida. As if I was hearing *my* name being called.'

'You seemed like a – like a ghost,' said Trewella.

'A ghost? Do you really think Davida's ghost is somewhere?'

Trewella shrugged.

'I doan't know. I came back to find out, I s'pose. I thought – 'twas a feelin' in me there might be somethin'. You see, girl, when people feel strongly about things, when they care enough, then their feelings carry over. Sometimes they leave them behind – sometimes, they do say, the very echoes can carry the sounds of voices that are silent, of laughter that's been stilled ...'

Karen clasped her hands together, her eyes shining.

'I can imagine that. Like the sea ...'

'What do 'ee know about the sea?'

'Only that I'm happier living here beside the sea than I've ever been in my whole life.'

'That – or happier living in this cottage?'

'Both, I think. They seem mixed up somehow. I don't feel satisfied until I get down to the sea. Every day I go along the shore and follow the curve of the bay. I take my shoes off and walk at the edge of the tide, smelling the seaweed and the salt and watching the little white crests of the waves racing in. Sometimes the waves come right over my feet, quick and cold – but exciting. I think to myself, the water that now washes my feet may once have lapped the shore of somewhere at the other end of the world. It's a marvellous thought.'

'Aye. The sea niver rests. It carries ships from one end of the earth to the other. Bodies, too. Sometimes a long, long way ... and they get swallowed up and niver seen again.'

'That must be awful. Is it a good way to die?'

Trewella shook his dark head firmly, with real passion.

'No, 'tis a terrible way. I was a fisherman, you know. I've had enough to do with the sea. I've seen it in all its moods and there's no pity, no love, no feeling. It's like the monsters that lurk in its depths. They just kill and devour, they doan't ask no questions and they give no answers. You asks any of the fishermen. They doan't want to die at sea. They want to die properlike in their own beds, on their own terms. I remembers a mate o' mine. We was out droppin' our pots and a squall came up. It was all over so quickly – we were nearly drove on to the rocks and we 'ad to pull sharp over. There was a wind came up from nowhere ... as if it had been waitin', hidin' round the corner until it could dart out and blow you into nothingness. That's what happened to this mate o' mine. What with the turn of the boat and the puff of wind, it caught him unawares and the boat rocked so much he went overboard into the sea. I shan't niver forget the look on his face. It was the look of a man who knew he was done for. I could niver get it out of my mind. He just – disappeared. We couldn't see to get hold of him, and then he was gone. All the way back all I could do was remember his face, the look on it. I could niver forget. And then I remembered it when –'

'When Davida was drowned?'

Karen jumped up, her face tense, her eyes filling as if with sudden tears.

'What is it?'

'I don't know. As you spoke, somehow I could see it all so very clearly. I feel as if I'm being pulled back into the past.'

Karen shuddered. Suddenly she got up and walked over to the far side of the room, shaking her head.

'Why do I have this feeling of familiarity?'

'You're like her, like Davida, that's all I know. When you said just then how you liked to walk along the sea – that's what she used to do. I've niver forgotten her, niver. I can't now. That's why I came back, that's the truth of it.'

'It frightens me.'

Trewella stared at her curiously.

'Why's that, girl? You says you're not Davida ...'

Karen made a wild, helpless gesture.

'You thought I was! How can anyone be sure? There are memories hanging around like – like raindrops waiting to fall. Can you feel them? I don't like the idea – I've always liked brightness and the sun.'

'So did she.'

'Stop it! Can't you see you're upsetting me? Oh, stop it, please!'

Suddenly Karen turned and ran over to the door and out. After making a half-hearted effort to stop her Trewella followed more slowly. For a moment he stood framed in the doorway, a shadowy figure: then he, too, disappeared.

5

Some time later Nora and Arnold Bruce arrived at the cottage. Nora went and called out for Richard but got no reply.

'He's probably gone for a walk on the cliffs,' said Bruce, obviously not displeased.

'You particularly wanted to see him, did you?'

'I must confess I'm in no hurry. I enjoy seeing his wife better.'

Nora smiled.

'Are you by any chance flirting with me?'

'Yes. Enjoying it too. Are you?'

She shrugged. 'Any woman likes to be flirted with. It proves she's still attractive.'

'Do you need such proof?'

'As much as any other woman.'

'But you're not quite as any other woman, are you? I mean, living here in this isolated cottage. It doesn't seem right to me. As soon as I saw you I felt you were a woman who needed her proper setting.'

'And this isn't it?'

Bruce gave her a searching look.

'No, it isn't. You must know that. Look, Mrs Eames – Nora – I'm a man of the world. I always believe in being honest. I would say you are a woman who has either made the wrong decision or shirked making one at all.'

He felt in his pocket and pulled out a silver case.

'Cigarette?'

'Thanks. Funny, I haven't smoked for quite some time. You seem to be stirring up old bad habits.'

Bruce laughed.

'Perhaps I can stir up a few more. I don't like to see a woman of charm and vitality living the life of a hermit. I feel it would do you good to be more your real self.'

Nora settled herself on the couch.

'Is that the real reason you want to stir up my old habits?'

Shrugging Bruce came over to offer a light. As he bent forward their eyes met. Suddenly, as if on abrupt decision, he leaned forward, took the cigarette out of Nora's mouth and kissed her.

'There – that's the reason. I wanted to do that from the moment I saw you. Did you know?'

'I had a premonition, shall we say.'

'Are you laughing at me?'

'Why should I? You're quite a formidable man.'

'I wouldn't mind if you were laughing. I could make you stop.'

'What, with money?'

'Yes, partly. I would certainly like to spend money on you, for you. To buy you clothes, hats, a string of luxuries you obviously haven't had for years.'

'Supposing that wasn't enough?'

'Of course it wouldn't be enough. But I could offer something else – a purpose, an aim in life. It could carry you along, I would take you with me. You would enjoy a new life.'

'But look at my husband. He has a purpose, I suppose – he's a writer.'

'And where has it got you? Perched here on the edge of the sea, away from the mainstream of life.'

Nora made a gesture.

'Yesterday you said your purpose was involved in coming here to this very spot you condemn. What's the difference between you and Richard?'

'For one thing I don't propose to bury myself here permanently – I'm only here as part of a process. In any case, there's all the difference in the world – the difference between reality and unreality. Your husband is weak, a dreamer, full of muddled ideas. What do they amount to? Can you see them? Can you feel them? I've told you what I'm going to do. It's real, it will take shape in front of your eyes, stone and cement, buildings, a whole pattern of reality. I tell you it's exciting. You don't get anything like that from your husband.'

With a sudden decisiveness Bruce sat beside Nora on the sofa. He took her hand and began stroking it gently.

'I like your independence. I can't bear subservient women.'

'How do you know I may not be such a woman?'

'I can see you're not,' said Bruce confidently. With the same confidence he pulled Nora's head against his shoulder and they settled down in comfortable proximity.

'But you know,' said Nora firmly. 'I must be subservient. I've lived such a life for the past twenty years. Before I was married I had many aims and ambitions. I was going to be a dress designer, had hopes about painting. I think it was the latter that partly attracted Richard to me. He probably thought it would make a romantic combination, two artists starving in a garret. But after marriage he realised, as I suppose most men do, that it would suit his convenience more to have a housekeeper. I must say I've been an efficient one, too. Twenty years in the same position – there's a testimony!'

'It's not the sort of life for you. You need adventure.'

'Isn't it a bit late? I'm forty-one you know.'

'I'm forty-eight, but I don't feel old.'

'You don't look old.'

'Nor do you. You just feel older because you've got into a groove, a dead end sort of life.'

'Don't talk like that!' exclaimed Nora with sudden, unexpected vehemence.

Bruce looked at her in surprise.

'It's true, isn't it?'

Nora turned her head away and he repeated the question. When she answered it was almost in a whisper.

'I don't know. Perhaps. That's why – I'd rather you didn't say it.'

Bruce looked at her averted head with compassion. All at once he bent forward and put his arms round Nora's shoulder, holding her firmly until at last, at first unwillingly and then more eagerly, she turned towards him.

'Nora ... My dear, let me help you. Let me bring some adventure into your life. You know I can.'

Suddenly Nora broke away, clambering to her feet and smoothing out her dishevelled dress.

'Someone's coming. Richard, I expect. Quick, sit over there.'

'All right. But promise we can meet, talk together ...?'

She smiled faintly.

'I promise.'

A moment later Richard came in through the door, seemingly unaware of any latent tension.

'Well, Mr Bruce, back to the attack, eh? I don't mind telling you I've been having all sorts of further thoughts, too. I mean about Martin and the cottage and all that.'

Bruce looked surprised.

'You mean you've changed your mind about selling?'

Richard gave him a pitying look.

'A mind with but a single thought ... How depressing. I do wish you would try and think beyond the confinements of your world and at least grant me the existence of my world. You see the advantage of my world is that it's limitless in time, in place, in space – in everything. Although admittedly I am at the moment here standing in Martin's Cottage, I'm not chained to the moment and the spot. There are other parts of me that can be ranging around in time and space. How often in fact have I stood here and looked around this room and with very little trouble I'm back in time – Martin's time. I like to imagine him here, walking round the room, coming down in the morning and lighting a fire, going over to the window and staring out to sea, his seaman's eye taking in the clouds and the currents, judging whether he should take the boat out fishing ...' As he spoke Richard began moving restlessly about the room.

'Martin himself, do you know, sometimes I see him quite clearly. A big man, I feel. Big and strong, dark, very dark – dark hair, a black beard. Eyes? I don't know, but I have the impression of bright, piercing eyes. An immensely powerful and determined man.'

'For all you know he might have been quite different, all shrivelled up,' interrupted Nora. 'Lots of the Cornish are.'

'Frankly I despise them,' said Bruce.

Richard turned on him. 'Yet you'd use them and their land for your profit?'

'I've told you, I'm a business man, not a sentimentalist. And anyway ...'

'And anyway what's my price, eh? Don't you realise I'm not interested? Why can't I make you *understand*? The fact is just being in this place can have a tremendous effect. Surely you can feel it?'

Bruce shook his head firmly.

'It's just another cottage.'

'Well then, Nora – *you* feel it, don't you?'

'Oh, Richard! I'm not in the mood for dreaming.'

'Karen does, anyway. I saw her not long ago going along the cliffs. She looked like something that *belonged*. She was hurrying, just like the wind hurries, and do you know I suddenly saw her as someone elemental, not quite of this world. Do you know, all my ideas seem to be falling into place. I walked down to the village with Miss Nicholas. When she had gone into her house I stood looking over the huddle of cottage roofs and blue smoke, then out at the bay, the little fishing boats bobbing about in the swell ... and then back at the cottage, standing like a sentinel over it all. Think how Martin must have liked that, the sensation of being above and beyond ordinary things, of being almost immortal. What it must have done to his character, how it must have moulded his thinking. Today I saw everything quite clearly, and just how I shall write about it. Not just an article, not just whimsy pieces, but a book, a novel, something permanent. Don't you see, that's why this place is so important to me. It's a creative challenge.'

Bruce gave a scornful laugh.

'Words, words! I'm a man of action myself.'

'Aha, deeds and not promises, eh? I wonder what action you would take if this was your place? I wonder if you would leave it alone or whether you might prefer to tear it down?'

For a moment Bruce looked angry.

'What do you mean? Why do you say that?'

'I just feel that probably there's something here in this cottage that you couldn't stand, that you wouldn't want to face up to. And – well, your way would be to obliterate, to exterminate.'

'I can be ruthless, I admit.'

'Does it always pay?'

'It always has done. Cut clean, it saves trouble – and the wound always heals in time.'

Bruce got to his feet.

'I'd better go now. I take it there's not much purpose in my attempting to discuss the cottage?'

'Not really,' said Richard. 'But there's no need to go. As a matter of fact, I'm in the mood to talk. My mind seems to be bursting with words and ideas ... images. It would be good to talk even to an opponent. Who knows, we might have a lot in common.'

Bruce, crossing to the door, paused and half turned. He gave Richard a long, penetrating look.

'Who knows indeed?'

As he went out of the door Nora began laughing, at first to herself, and then quite openly – strained and unnatural laughter that she could not seem to stop. 'What is it?' said Richard at last. 'Nora, what is it?'

But Nora just laughed.

6

One day not long after, taking a long walk along the cliffs, Karen met Alan, the lighthousekeeper, and persuaded him to come back with her to the cottage. He seemed diffident about accompanying her but in the end followed her up the steps and stood hesitantly at the entrance to the big sitting room.

'At least come in,' said Karen with a flash of impatience. 'I should have thought even if you don't like Martin's Cottage you'd be glad of a chance to see it from inside.'

'I can look at it from outside – that's enough for me.'

Alan moved over to the fireplace and stood looking around.

'I never thought I'd ever stand here, because of something my father said years ago when I was a child. It quite frightened me ... and then that day I met you on the cliffs and we started talking, you seemed so nice and sweet it made me feel the cottage couldn't be a bad place after all.' He looked around and shook his head doubtfully. 'But now that I'm here it all seems to come back to me.'

'What *did* your father tell you?'

'He said that Martin was like a spider and that anyone who came into his power would never get away again – yes, that was it, I remember.'

'I don't believe Martin can have been like that at all. Why, when I think of Martin I just feel sad. He must have been so lonely ...'

Alan went on doggedly.

'There must have been something in what my father said. Others will tell you the same. Martin did like keeping things to himself. He would never let anyone else use his boat – he'd fly into a real temper if any of the children went near. Everything he owned – his donkey, his dog, even the hens he kept – he kept them shut away from people, just like himself. And then there was this place, his home – 'twas always *Martin's* Cottage, no one else's.'

'Well, I don't care what your father says. I feel at home here.'

'Are you sure? You don't seem quite the same as out there on the cliffs. There's something. You're not so – free.'

Karen shrugged impatiently.

'Of course I'm free. It's just that – well, it's my father's fault really. He goes on and on harping on the strange history of this place that in the end he makes you feel nothing else is important in the whole world.'

'I expect that's how Martin used to think. Nothing else mattering, only his own little world. It's easy to get like that. It's the same when I'm on duty at the lighthouse. Cut off, the sea everywhere, the sense of being trapped – it's easy to believe there's nowhere else in the world.'

Karen nodded.

'Yes, that's it. The longer I'm here the more I feel I'm becoming a part of the cottage. And then, well, it's more than that. That man coming back – feeling almost as if I've known him before ...'

'I've never even seen him yet.'

'That's just it – he's so secretive. He's never been down to the village. You'd think he would, for old times' sake. But he says he hasn't come back to see the village.'

'Then why?'

When Karen did not answer Alan gave a sudden shiver.

'I don't like it here. Please ... let's go out again, on to the cliffs.' He looked upset. 'This place has a strange effect on you. I can imagine it changing you, making you into – another person. Changing you so much that I wouldn't know you any more.'

While Alan was talking the door opened upstairs and Richard came slowly down, listening to the last few sentences with approval.

'A young man of some imagination! That's a fascinating idea.'

Karen gestured.

'I wanted Alan to see Martin's Cottage but he doesn't seem to like it very much. Isn't he silly?'

Richard grimaced.

'Well, there's no doubt the place does have a strong atmosphere. It might put off some people. You and I, perhaps we're more in tune with it. I know what I want from this cottage – atmosphere, revelation, mystery. It's all here.'

He looked at Alan inquiringly so that the young man seemed impelled to answer.

'People have never stayed here long, you know.'

'Oh, I know all about those stories,' said Richard. 'They don't bother me.' He shrugged. 'You work in the lighthouse, don't you? It must be a strange job. How long are you out there?'

'Two months on, one month ashore.'

'I don't envy you. Surely you must get on each other's nerves?'

'It's not too bad – at least it leaves you time to think. And then you do appreciate things more when you come on land again. Like flowers and grass, the heather on the cliffs.' He looked shyly at Karen. 'That's why I like walking along the cliffs. They're something like the rocks where the lighthouse stands – and yet so different. The rocks are cold and bare, nothing grows on them, the sea washes everything away. But the cliffs – they're alive with things that grow. I love to sit and look around me ...' He looked appealingly at Karen. 'Are you sure you wouldn't like to come out for a walk?'

When Karen shook her head Alan went over to the door and

out down the steps. Karen went and watched him from the window and then turned and leaned back, staring dreamily into space.

'Penny for them,' said Richard with a smile.

'I was thinking about lighthouses – and how this place might almost be one, really. Should we be so cut off, do you think?'

Richard reflected.

'I only know I've never worked so well as since I came here. It's as if something's been released in me. Of course if what was released was something *bad*, a devil or something like that, well, I don't know what I'd say then.'

'It suddenly struck me when you asked Alan if being cooped up didn't make people get on each other's nerves – do you know ever since we've been here, you and I – and Mother – we've become different people.'

Richard laughed.

'Do I have green ears and horns coming out of my head?'

'Not that sort of change – but, yes, you have changed, the way you look at things, the way you think ...'

Karen spread her hands out in front of her.

'It affects us each differently, I suppose. When we first came here I felt so very happy. And yet it wasn't an ordinary sort of happiness, it was almost as if it were – well, you'll think I'm silly, I suppose – but stolen. Borrowed if you like – borrowed happiness. More as if I were playing a part rather than experiencing something new.'

Richard stared at his daughter. How strange she looked as she talked, he thought. He felt a tremor of unknown fear.

'And now,' Karen went on, 'the awful thing is I'm aware of unhappiness – a sense of it, anyway, of it impending.'

'It doesn't sound like you.'

'That's what frightens me. The thought, even the suspicion that – that – '

'What are you getting at?'

Karen sank down on to the couch, bowing her head.

'You'll think I'm being hysterical ... but it keeps coming back to me, the memory of that man looking up and his voice crying out across a great distance, crying out that name. It sounded so familiar. Oh, how I wish we could somehow press a button and go back in time, see what really did happen here all those years ago, the time of Davida and Martin and all their problems. If only we knew ...'

Just as Karen was finishing talking there was a tap at the door and Trewella appeared. Richard made a welcoming gesture.

'The very man. You will tell her, won't you, Trewella? All about Martin and Davida, what happened.'

Trewella hesitated.

'Tongues wag in Cornwall like nowhere else, I can tell you. I've had plenty of that in my time.'

'Did they wag about Martin?'

'Martin? Yes, and well they might.'

'Did he do you some harm, then?'

'Many people didn't like Martin, but I suppose I had the most cause of all. You see ... well, he wasn't like other men, not really.'

Richard made a gesture.

'He must have had a mother and a father and gone to school and all that?'

Trewella shook his head.

'That's just it; he had no mother and father. He was an orphan, a little stray waif of a boy that an old fisherman picked up one night in the streets of Penzance. You'll understand that in those times there wasn't the same efficiency about looking after stray children. This old fisherman, Ben Nicholas he was called, he took a fancy to the boy, I suppose, just like you or I might take a fancy to a stray kitten, and he brought him home to his place in the village. It were a strange combination the old, old man and the young, young boy. Ole Ben Nicholas had lived on his own all his life; odd you might say that he should suddenly want a companion. Not that Martin was much of a companion. He was always down on the beach or climbing the cliffs for birds' eggs. He'd go out with Ben on the boats though ... yes, because he wanted to learn all about them and how to fish. He used to go out with Ben sometimes when the sea was so rough it was like a boiling cauldron. Ben was an old man and perhaps he didn't fear any more, as for Martin – well if he had any fear in him it must have been blown away by the winds and the storms. Yes, I reckon that before he was fifteen Martin had faced death a dozen times. But you'll understand that a man who feared nothing, not even death – well, he became a hard man, not the sort to feel pity or tenderness or – '

'Love?' said Richard.

'Love? Why do you mention love?'

'But the girl Davida – I thought you said Martin loved her.'

'Maybe ... and maybe not.'

There was silence for a while, stretching so long that Richard felt impelled to break it.

'Were you friends, like you said?'

Trewella nodded.

'Yes. After the old man died we became friends. Sometimes I used to help him build this cottage. I can remember it all. I'll never forget it to my dying day, the way it took shape, stone upon stone, the walls rising up out of the earth and rock. Sometimes the wind freshened and a gale blew and there was rain for hours on end ... you'd have thought the stones would all be washed away but they stood. There was somethin' strong and lastin' about the cottage even then. You could feel it, standin' there among all the heaps o' stones and the half-finished walls. You could hear the wind howlin' round and pokin' into holes and round corners as if it wanted to blow everything away. But it never did. The walls grew higher and stronger, the beams went up for the roof, and at last the grey-blue slates were laid in rows, shuttin' out the rain and the wind ... and the sun.'

'Oh, yes,' said Karen excitedly. 'I can see it all happening.'

'When it was all finished,' Trewella went on, 'Martin left the village and came up here and lived alone. He was always alone – him and his cottage. He was some proud of this place. Every inch of it belonged to him, he said. I don't think he ever felt lonely in this place. 'Twas Martin's Cottage, allus would be, he said. I s'pose he got a bit strange, livin' here all alone. It makes a person strange, you know, being alone. I've been alone for weeks on end in Africa, just wanderin' and sleepin' … you get ideas, dreams, memories, all jumbled up. You niver know whether you're alive or dead. Sometimes you're back in childhood, schooldays, youthful days … '

'But you were his friend,' said Richard. 'You must have been with him a lot?'

Trewella looked up, a curious expression crossing his dark face.

'Haven't you heard the gossip then? How Martin and John Trewella loved the same woman? How two friends were turned into two enemies?'

'Because of – Davida?'

'Aye. There was so much alike about the two of them they were bound to be drawn. She was such a waif-like thing she always looked as if she had come out of the seas and was looking for something … you wanted to help her.'

'And Martin felt that?'

'He couldn't seem to take his eyes away from her. He used to sit on the cliffs looking down to where she was walking along the beach road, or sitting in her father's garden. She used to serve in Mrs Stevens' shop and often Martin would come and stand outside staring through the window. You'd have thought she would have been angry but she weren't.'

Richard looked puzzled.

'But I thought she was your girl?'

Trewella smiled grimly.

'Aye, she were my girl, my Davida. All mine. Though I'm damned if I know how you can possess that which no longer exists.' He paused, and suddenly gave a long look at Karen. 'Or perhaps you can, who knows?' He shook his head. 'People don't have the imagination …'

'What's wrong, Karen?' said Richard in sudden concern. 'You're shivering. Are you all right?'

'She's frightened,' said Trewella. 'Just like Davida used to be. It's the same restlessness … the same. I can remember Davida standing by the window and walkin' about and claspin' her hands like she was an animal before a storm, jumpy and tense, without peace.'

Richard suddenly felt angry.

'Well, she's certainly disturbed and it's your fault. You really mustn't upset her like this.'

''Tis not I who upset her. Is it, me dear?'

At his searching look Karen became more restless, clasping and unclasping her hands.

'I'm not Davida – am I, Father?'

'No, of course not. Such rubbish!' said Richard, still angry.

Karen sighed.

'That's the sort of thing Mother would say. She sees things cut and dried, black and white. She will always choose the most sensible course. She will make her own life. But you're not like her, Father. When you say "Such rubbish" you don't really mean it. You are more like me really, a part of you wants to believe in the unbelievable, to penetrate the impenetrable. You have faith in the myths.'

Richard nodded. 'Perhaps you're right. Perhaps all life is a myth? No time, no place, no movement – us and now, Martin and the past, all mixed up, all still here, colouring the air, spreading tentacles around us, binding. Yes.' Caught up in the magic of his thoughts Richard rambled on: 'I wonder – I wonder if it's really that in Cornwall the gap doesn't exist between reality and unreality?'

On an impulse he crossed over and put a shyly protective arm around Karen.

'My dear, you know I've always loved you in a way I've never loved anyone else!'

Karen sighed.

'Then you'll have to try and understand me if ...'

'If what?'

Trewella, staring at Karen steadily, gave the answer.

'If she goes away.'

Karen gave a shudder and put her hands to her face.

'He thinks he knows everything because it has happened before.'

She turned and buried herself in her father's arms. Richard turned angrily on the Cornishman.

'I think you'd better go.'

'Aye,' said Trewella. 'But you'll remember 'twas you who asked me to tell you about Martin. You asked me an' I told you.'

'You told us something – not everything. I still don't have a clear picture of Martin.'

Trewella shrugged.

'Perhaps you never will. Perhaps no one ever did.' He paused and looked hard at Karen. 'But then some did ... yes, some did.'

'For heaven's sake,' exclaimed Richard. 'You'll make her cry.'

'Cry?' Trewella rose to his feet, agitated. 'Oh, me dear, doan't cry. This is no time for tears.'

He paused, as if preparing to move forward – then, changing his mind, turned and went over to the door. Looking suddenly dejected, he went out. Richard crossed to the window and watched as the dark Cornishman went steadily down the long, winding steps. There was something strange about his journey, a finality. At the bottom, instead of turning towards the village he took the grassy footpath that led out to the open cliffs.

'I don't like it,' said Karen. She had come and stood behind Richard, following his gaze. 'The way he came and went so – so finally.'

'A strange man.' Richard shook his head. 'Suddenly he arrives out of nowhere from thousands of miles ... becomes part of our life, the whole of our life ... And then in a flash, now as he walks away, perhaps he is disappearing forever again.'

'Father – no!'

He swung round, contrite.

'I was only thinking aloud – it's only my writer's imagination. Look, there he is still there, climbing up the cliffs.'

'You don't understand. I *know* now. That's why he came back and told us – he'll never come back ... and I shall never know. Oh, Father, look – in a minute he will be beyond that carn, out of sight forever.'

She swung round agitatedly.

'I must go and catch him up before it's too late.'

'Karen!' cried Richard. 'No, Karen, please ...'

But he was too late, he could only watch from the door as the familiar figure of his daughter rushed down the steps like a whirlwind down and down and then far out along the distant cliffs.

7

Nora had been a long while making up her mind, but once she had done so she acted swiftly. Up in her bedroom she took down a large suitcase and packed it with clothes, squeezing it shut with some difficulty, and then carrying it down into the sitting room. She put down the case and went to take down her coat and hat from the hallstand. She turned intending to pick up the case and walk to the doorway – but suddenly there was a sound and Richard came in.

He looked across at Nora rather vaguely.

'I've been looking for Karen. I'm worried. She went out on to the cliffs.'

'She's often gone out on the cliffs. I hardly think she'll come to any harm.'

'What is it?' Richard interrupted suddenly, seeing the suitcase. 'Where are you going?'

Nora paused and then spoke in a low, controlled voice.

'How long have we been married?'

'I don't know – a good many years. I haven't thought about it really.'

'That's just it. You've thought about your work, about words, about fantasies, little worlds of your own ... but not about your marriage.'

'What's wrong? What's the matter?'

'The matter is myself – my life with you. For years I've gone about in a sort of fog, not thinking. I've followed you around, cooking for you, looking after you and Karen, keeping a home together, trying to make ends meet. I suppose I got into the habit of it. It's only when we came here to this cottage that I began to wake up to the sort of drudgery of a life that was mine.'

'You can't mean that?'

'You'll never understand, will you? You've always lived in a world of your own, a world of words.'

'But words are my living!'

'What a living! Scraping for every penny – how we've managed to exist for so long I don't know. Now here we are at the end of the world. What will happen? You're not earning anything.'

'Not yet, but I am *planning* something – immense. I've told you, this place is a stimulus. It will help me to write something great. I know, I'm sure.'

'Well, I'm not sure – not about that. What I am sure about is that I can't stand it any longer, this half-existence. When did you last buy me a new dress? Or anything? Most men would make some effort to find the cash, to give their wives a little happiness.'

Richard looked bewildered.

'It's no good.' Nora shook her head. 'I thought perhaps I could explain, but it's a waste of time.'

She put the coat over her arm and bent down and picked up the case.

'But where are you going?'

'I'm going to do something *new*. I'm going to step out of my rut. You can have Martin's Cottage. I don't want any part of it. As far as I'm concerned it's like your words, a myth, a dead end. I want to go out into the sunshine and begin to live before it's too late.'

'What about me?'

'You've got Martin's Cottage. That's what you want, isn't it? You just want to sit here and play with words. As for me – I'd rather play with life, even if I get hurt.'

As Nora moved towards the door Richard half raised a hand in protest, then dropped it.

'You're really going? Alone?'

At the door Nora paused, turning defiantly.

'No, I'm not young enough for that. I haven't the strength to begin again alone.'

Richard gave an exclamation.

'Not Bruce? Not that money-bags?'

'He's more than that. He's a kind man in his way. And a lonely one. Someone who probably needs me more than you for all his money.'

'What nonsense! He's buying you just like he wanted to buy the cottage. Can't you see?'

'Put it like that if you want. Well, you can keep your cottage. He can manage without it, I'm sure.' She paused, halfway through the door, and said in a low voice. 'Goodbye, Richard ...' Then she was gone.

Still standing in the middle of the room, both arms half raised despairingly, Richard felt as if he was chained to the ground. A part of him could not believe what was happening, another part attempted helplessly to juggle with other problems. In a low monotone he began talking to himself.

'That must have been what's been in the air, a sort of premonition ... So you've gone, Nora. Gone to Bruce and all his money. Very well, buy your happiness ... It's true what you said, I've got the cottage. I can write, make new worlds, why should I worry?' He paused, and then stumbled on. 'As long as Karen's all right.'

He peered out of the window, staring intensely for several moments, hoping against hope ... but when suddenly at last his eyes caught a movement it was not Karen, but a glimpse of two people coming up the steps towards the cottage. A moment later he went and opened the door to the Reverend Lanyon and Alan, both looking agitated.

'My dear fellow,' said the vicar, out of breath. 'We came at once. A terrible thing ...'

'What is it?'

'It's Karen,' said Alan. 'We're afraid of what might have happened to her. You see, earlier this evening I saw her running along the cliffs.'

'That's right. She went after that fellow Trewella.'

'Well, I called out but she didn't reply. I thought maybe she was still cross with me. We had a bit of a quarrel earlier, you see. So after a while I decided to go after her. The trouble is there was this sea mist coming in and it was beginning to settle on the cliffs ... somehow I just lost track of her.'

'The cliffs? You mean – she's fallen?'

Alan shook his head.

'No, I followed the path over the cliffs and then down to Treganton Cove. There are some boats kept there, pulled up on the beach. One of them was gone – she must have taken it. Matter of fact I did have half an idea I saw the shape of a boat disappearing into the mist but I couldn't be sure. I called out after it but there was no reply ... I just heard my voice echoing amongst the rocks.'

The vicar cleared his throat.

'I'm afraid there's something else. About half an hour ago two of the fishermen came back. They were towing a boat. It was the one missing from Treganton.'

'The same one,' exclaimed Alan. 'It was choppy, the currents and the swell would have made it difficult – she must have fallen overboard. Leastways, that's what they think. The boat hadn't capsized or anything, it was just drifting.'

Richard gave a cry.

'My God, Karen! We must search for her – at once, before it's too late.'

The vicar put out a restraining hand.

'Calm yourself. That's already being done. Three boats have gone out – they're all experienced fishermen, there couldn't be anyone better. If she can possibly be found she will be.' He sighed. 'The ways of the Lord are strange.'

'The ways of the Lord!' exclaimed Richard. 'This is beyond that, I can tell you. This is the work of the Devil, not the Lord.'

As Richard suddenly sat down, burying his face in his hands, Alan went over to the window.

'I told her to leave here,' he said dully.

'That's what I mean,' said Richard, to the vicar. 'He knows, the boy knows. It's the Devil's work. This cottage. Martin's Cottage ... My God, fool that I've been. Why didn't I recognise it? The evil side of it all ...'

Alan turned from the window.

'Nobody would come near this cottage for years. I can remember when I was a boy, we used to pass over the cliffs going to school and all of us were frightened. You've no idea how weird the cottage would look silhouetted against the dying sky. Gaunt and weird.'

The vicar made a movement.

'Martin was rather like that,' he said. 'Gaunt and weird. I suppose you *could* say he might have given the impression of carrying within him some sort of evil spirit. But it's wrong to bow before it, Mr Eames. We must trust in God.'

Richard shook his head.

'This is beyond that. Don't you see? This is bound up with the granite walls of this cottage, mixed with the sand and cement that weld it together, hidden in the beams and joists, lurking behind every doorway, in the shadow of every corner, upstairs among the rafters ... the power of a man's mind. Why, I felt it the day I first crossed this threshold – only then I couldn't define it, I was simply aware of the atmosphere, the whole cottage breathing the life of the past, this faraway link with that distant personality. I suppose I became a little possessed. Perhaps there was something of Martin that got into me, making me think I was a strong man who was going to write a great book.' He bowed his head. 'Not a man whose life was going to be broken into tiny fragments in the hollow shell of this – this *cursed* cottage.'

Alan was looking out of the window again.

'The mist is rising at last. We might still have some evening light before the sun sinks.'

He turned away.

'I feel so ill at ease here ... Do you, Mr Lanyon?'

The vicar shook his head.

'I have my faith to sustain me, you see. I may feel lost and terrified, but I never give up hope. I have always had faith.'

Richard began musing aloud.

'Martin must have had a faith of his own. Something immensely strong and powerful to keep him going. A faith in his cottage.'

Alan shivered.

'A dark and terrible place.'

'But to Martin no doubt an oasis of peace,' said the vicar.

Richard looked about wildly.

'Do you really imagine there can have been peace in a place so alive with such passions and torments? Why, even now one can sense them, the strange undercurrents – as if some will is trying to get rid of us. Oh yes, I can feel it all – now, when it's too late. I thought I could be clever, I thought I could utilise those forces to my own advantage, but I realise now they are too powerful.'

He began moving distraughtly about the room.

'Karen's the only one who really felt and understood, the only one close enough to the elements. She realised how even over all those years a man's mind could still keep control of that which it created.'

'For goodness sake – let's go,' said Alan. He took Richard's arm anxiously.

'Come along, Mr Eames. You can't stay here. Come with us.'

Richard nodded.

'Yes, you're right.'

He began to move towards the door and then as if struck by a thought turned back, looking upwards. His voice rose to a high note as he began shouting out.

'Very well, Martin – you can have your way! Can you hear me, Martin?'

'For Heaven's sake,' said the vicar agitatedly. 'Stop it.'

'I'm talking to you, Martin!' Richard gave a hollow laugh. 'I know you're here somewhere. I know you've *always* been here somewhere, like some great, ugly shadow. I might have guessed that you'd be hating intruders, willing us to go. Well, you'll have your way ...'

'Come on,' said Alan firmly.

At the doorway he paused.

'Look, the mist has risen and see – the boats are returning. The three of them. You can see them drawing towards the harbour.'

'Oh, God,' said Richard. 'Can you see anything else?'

'No, it's too far away.'

The vicar moved forward resolutely.

'There's always hope. Come along, we'll go and meet them.'

The three of them went out of the door and down the steps, leaving the door swinging behind them – as they did so there could be heard the whistle of the wind and the boom of the waves. Suddenly it seemed as if the wind gathered force and blew its way through the doorway and into the room, bringing with it a strange sense of desolation.

Across in the kitchen there was a sudden sound of movements. Slowly the kitchen door opened and Trewella entered, leading Karen by the hand. They were both bedraggled and wet, Karen with her long hair hanging down, looking wild and dishevelled. She seemed to hesitate, hanging back, taking each step almost unwillingly. Trewella turned and beckoned her on, into the centre of the room. When at last Karen stood there she seemed uncertain as if she was partaking of a dream.

With quick movements Trewella went around closing the windows, closing the door, shutting up the shutters, drawing the curtains, then lighting up the lamp on the centre table. Everything he did was done expertly, with an air of familiarity.

Coming back to the centre of the room he took Karen by both hands.

'Wake up, me dear, wake up to our world we've waited for so long.'

Karen shivered looking round curiously as if in some way she was seeing the cottage for the first time.

'I feel so cold, cold, all the way through. As if I'd been turned into stone.'

'But you're not turned into stone – you've become alive – alive forever!'

'I don't know whether I'm alive or … I recognise my

surroundings and yet they aren't the same as before. They seem further away – and yet, strangely, more familiar than ever.'

'You're home, me dear, *home*.'

'Am I really?'

As she spoke Karen looked across at Trewella.

'When I heard you calling me ... down there in the cold sea ... your voice sounded as if it was calling from such a long way away ... and so tired, such a tired voice, like it had been calling and calling. Do you know, when I heard that voice I didn't mind then if I drowned, it didn't seem to matter. I was happy because I heard your voice, Trewella.'

'Ah,' said Trewella. 'But 'twasn't Trewella's voice you heard. Do you understand, me dear? The real Trewella died many years ago, died far from here in the blisterin' sun of Africa ...'

'Then who – ?'

Trewella made a sudden movement, his arms outstretched.

'Who do 'ee think, Davida? Who told you 'ee would love you to the end of time? Who knelt and kissed the ground you walked on? Who followed you round like the lost stray dog he once was? Who – tell me, Davida, love of my life.'

Karen put a hand to her mouth, her eyes widening.

'Martin ...?'

'Aye, Martin, the lonely fisherman ... the sad lover ... the man who built this cottage with his bare hands ... the man who loved Davida so much that he denied her death and willed her life, that he held her in his heart across all the years long after he was lost in the deep sea.'

'But that was so many years ago ... My name isn't Davida ...'

'Years! What are years? What are names? What is time? How do you know any of these things ever existed? 'Tis love that matters – love that niver dies. You knows in your heart who's always loved, loves! Isn't it there, that feelin', Davida – or no Davida?'

Karen began rocking from side to side.

'Oh, my head's spinning! I feel as I felt when the boat

rocked and I fell into the water, deep down into the water, as if the world had slipped away from under my feet and I was floating in nothingness, into a strange and beautiful dream.' She looked wonderingly at Trewella. 'And if it's a dream, then perhaps I *am* Davida ...'

'Listen to the wind, Davida! Listen to the wind howlin' from the cliffs. Think of it lashin' the waves and whippin' them into a frenzy – think of it hurryin' above the clouds, blowin' them down upon us like angry men ... 'Twill be a wild night tonight. The cliffs will be blistered with rain, the beach groanin' under the weight of great boomin' waves – the houses and cottages will rattle and tremble and people will be glad to shut themselves away in their little rooms and huddle around their fires. But us, Davida, them that come out of the deep sea, us shan't have to hide any more. The wind and the rain and the sea can't harm us now.'

He made a gesture around the cottage, proud, possessive.

''Tis safe here, my darling, safe in Martin's Cottage. 'Twas built for you and me, my sweetheart.'

Suddenly Karen stretched herself, as if awakening to some new reality.

'Oh, Martin! I feel a great wave of happiness – I feel alive!'

Impetuously she half walked, half danced round the room. As she did so Trewella watched her lovingly, knowingly – and indeed she seemed in some strange way to be almost another person.

'Martin, is this what it feels to be really alive? This warmth that steals over me like a loving hand – this bursting, wonderful joy that swells up inside me so that I feel my heart will break? Is this being alive?'

'Alive ... or ... dead. Sleepin' ... wakin' ... livin' ... dreamin'. We are free of it all now, me dear. Free as the birds on the wing.'

'Somehow I don't feel afraid anymore. I know that I belong here – for ever and ever.'

'We both do, Davida – we're part of the stones and the beams and walls, part of this cottage.

Suddenly Karen stepped to the window: outside the light had faded into dusk. She pointed downwards 'Look, there are little lights coming up the steps. Just like fairy lights. What can they be? Why are they coming here?'

Trewella went and stood behind her.

'They're lanterns, me dear. Fishermen's lanterns – but we don't need to worry about them no more. They will go on gropin' around in the dark, lightin' a corner here and a corner there ... but we're beyond their reach, Davida. We don't need lonely lanterns – see over there – there's sunshine for us.'

Karen clasped her hands together, her face lighting up. When the two of them stared out of the window it was as if into some great distance away, far beyond the mere mortals carrying lanterns below.

'I see sunshine,' said Karen. 'I see blue sky and green cliffs and white seagulls wheeling round and round ... Oh, Martin, let us go out into the sunshine.'

She took Trewella's arm. Mysteriously, almost imperceptibly, they seemed to glide through the doorway and into their other world ... as they went so it seemed for a moment as if the wind became stilled and the sound of the sea receded, and for a moment even the light outside noticeably brightened.

8

When the light had dimmed again there began to appear the dancing gleam of the fishermen's lanterns coming nearer and nearer to the cottage, the sound of heavy, booted feet clambering up the steps. At last the door handle rattled and there entered a small procession: first the Reverend Lanyon who held the door open, and then behind him Richard, his face transfigured with grief, carrying in his arms the limp sea-washed body of Karen, her head hanging down so that her long dark hair brushed the ground below. Carefully Richard carried the body over to the couch and laid it down gently.

As Alan also came into the room the vicar went over to the door and spoke to the fishermen outside, thanking them for their help, telling them there was nothing more they could do now and they should go back to their beds.

When the fishermen had gone he shut the door and turned back into the room.

'Strange that they should find the girl but no sign of Trewella,' he said. 'Yet he seems to have disappeared just as completely as if he had been drowned too.'

Richard shook his head dazedly.

'I'm beginning to feel he was never here, that he was always a drowned man, the whole thing a dream —' He bent down and gently brushed away the flowing, dark hair from Karen's pale forehead. 'Ah, but it's no dream, it's a nightmare. Oh, Karen my love, how still and cold you are.'

'Poor child,' said the vicar compassionately.

'That's how she always seemed to me,' said Richard. 'A child — she never quite grew up.'

The vicar nodded.

'Often they are the happiest, the children who never quite grow up.'

Alan interrupted, speaking quietly.

'She was young in some ways, old in others. Older than any of us perhaps.'

Richard sank down on the side of the couch, looking slowly round the cottage and shaking his head in bewilderment.

'It's only a few days since I sat in this very room and wondered what influence Martin's Cottage might have on our lives. Now I suppose the eternal pattern will go on. Someone else will sit here and feel the strangeness that we felt, some other family will look at these solid walls and think about the past. Perhaps one of them will feel the still warm tears ... or the cold touch of Karen's poor dead hand.'

He shook his head in desolation.

'I shall go away and never see this place again. I shall even try and forget it. But Martin — Martin has never forgotten it!'

He looked down sorrowfully at his forever sleeping daughter.

'Poor Karen, what use are my words now? They cannot bring you back. Nothing can bring you back.'

He paused, looking helplessly from the vicar to Alan. In the end it was Alan who spoke.

'See what a strange look of peace there is upon her face! Look, there's a faint smile at the corner of her lips ... and her eyes are closed so peacefully, her forehead so smooth and untroubled.'

'Yes,' said Richard. 'She looks almost happy. As if – as if she has found something wonderful and marvellous.'

Alan nodded.

'I'll tell you – she looks like she looked that afternoon on the cliffs when I first met her. I shall always remember – the sun was shining and the sky was deep blue and the seagulls were circling overhead ... She threw her head back and the wind lifted her hair up so that it streamed out behind her. I remember clearly what she said. She said, "I shall always be happy here, always." And then I can remember she said something else. She said, "You know, it's not just Martin's Cottage – it's *mine*, too."' He paused, his voice almost a whisper. 'I think perhaps now it is ...'

In the silence that followed the three men looked at one another uneasily as if aware for a moment not merely of the fourth occupant lying upon the couch but perhaps of some other presence, lurking in the shadows, waiting only for their departure. And so they remained for a long, long time.

II

Boy Missing

Johnny decided to run away that very night. He would wait until the other boys in the dormitory were asleep and it was all dark and quiet. Then he would get up, put on his clothes, stuff his precious few belongings into his pocket, and creep away.

Once the decision had been made, somehow he felt eased in his mind. It made more bearable all the things that caused him to feel so desperate and miserable: wandering forlornly around the school yard, queuing up for tea, sitting in the classroom doing homework while outside the late sunshine beckoned invitingly. It was his first week at boarding school, his first week away from familiarity and security – and he hated it, he hated every single moment of it.

So he was going to escape from it all. It was an exciting, even an inspiring thought. Johnny did not really think beyond it: he had no clear idea where he would go. It seemed enough that he would free himself from this – this prison. And that thought alone gave him a warm sense inside, so that for the remainder of the day he went about with a secret, knowing smile on his round face.

He didn't even mind the usual ragging, the other boys splashing water at him in the bathroom, finding his bed made up in traditional apple-pie style. Blake did that, he supposed, the tall boy in the bed next to him, who seemed ever ready to get in a dig. Well, all right, Blake, enjoy your joke for the very last time, he thought.

He undressed and got into bed, secure with his secret. None of the usual jeers could penetrate his peace of mind. Go on, he thought, talk away, laugh if you like. Just you wait and see – in the morning, why, you'll find you're talking to yourselves.

And he lay back in bed, hands behind his head, staring up at the white-washed ceiling, contemplating the drama of his disappearance. He imagined the first discovery, the boys searching, then one of them going off to tell old Sampson, the housemaster, then a flurry of official inquiries until finally the Head himself was informed. And then – why, then perhaps it would be in all the newspapers, maybe on the radio. He could almost imagine the big headlines: SCHOOL MYSTERY – BOY DISAPPEARS.

Mind you, he'd be sorry to upset old Sampson. Somehow he felt more at ease with the elderly white-haired housemaster than with the others. He hadn't been like the Head, all bustle and fuss and discipline. Old Sampson had a sort of friendly look in his eyes. He didn't seem to stare through you like some of the masters – rather did he seem to be very much aware of you, looking deep into your heart.

Ah well, sighed Johnny. It couldn't be helped. Perhaps old Sampson at least, if nobody else, would understand why he just had to go.

For a long time Johnny lay still and quiet, listening for the breathing of his companions. Every now and then he heard the striking of the church clock across the road. Ten, ten-fifteen, ten-thirty.

At last he decided the other boys were asleep, must be asleep. Indeed, it had been all he could do to keep awake himself. But now, faced with the reality of his actions, he was suddenly wide awake.

Stealthily, he got out of bed and put on his clothes. Pausing to fold back the bedclothes and hump up a pillow to give the impression of a sleeping form, he turned and crept down the centre of the long dormitory.

At the top of the staircase he paused. All was in darkness, and though there was some light from the moon through the main window, it was all rather eerie.

Still, it was too late now. Holding his breath Johnny tiptoed down the stairs and out of the main door into the garden.

Outside, all was quiet. Somewhere he heard the lonely echo of an owl hooting. He shivered, feeling suddenly more alone than he had ever imagined. He looked around nervously, seeing shapes and shadows everywhere. Well, come on now, no good giving way to imagination. He knew what he was going to do, he had worked it all out: he was going to the railway station to catch the last train up to London.

Then – well after that he hadn't thought, really. It seemed enough, first, to get away from the school. London was such a big place, they would never find him there. Whereas, if they went straight to his home – why, of course, that was the first place they would inquire at. And the trouble was he couldn't feel absolutely sure about his parents. He couldn't help feeling that though they might not be angry, they might want him to go back.

So London it must be. He felt in his pocket, where he kept the four pound notes he had been given to start off the term with – London wasn't very far, he didn't expect it would cost more than one of those notes. On the rest he ought to be able to manage for quite a while.

Walking along the streets leading to the station he felt very conscious of his loneliness, hearing the sound of his footsteps echoing loudly – too loudly, really. He bent his head down and tried to melt into the shadows.

At the station he approached the ticket office, and then lost his nerve. It had not occurred to him before but they were bound to think it rather strange for a small boy to buy a ticket to London at that time of night. No, he couldn't afford the risk. He hesitated, looking around. How should he get on the platform?

In the distance he heard the sound of a train coming from London. When it stopped and the people were coming off, the ticket-inspector's attention would be occupied – that would be the time to nip on to the platform. Then he would go over to the up-platform on the other side, when all was quiet again, and wait for the last train.

When the London train pulled in Johnny was waiting in the shadows. As soon as passengers started coming off he climbed over the stone wall and found himself on the platform. All the time his eyes had been focussed on the lighted exit where the collector stood, taking tickets.

Consequently Johnny did not notice that one passenger had got out of one of the front carriages rather later than most of the others, and was now walking down past where he crouched. In fact, so near that he almost fell over Johnny, who gave a startled gasp.

'Bless my soul!' came a voice, a familiar voice, out of the darkness. 'And what exactly is all this about?'

At the sound of the familiar voice Johnny turned to run, but he was too late. A hand fell on his shoulder, and he was swung around.

'So,' said the one and only voice of Mr Sampson, 'it's you, the new boy, eh? And where do you think you're going at this time of night?'

Johnny swallowed hard.

'Sir, I was going – to London.'

The old man raised his bushy eyebrows.

'Well, indeed, isn't that a coincidence? I've just come from London, and you're just going. Have you got your ticket?'

'Er, no, sir. You see ...'

'I know, I know. You don't have to explain the details, boy. I was your age once myself, though you may find it hard to believe.' There was the suspicion of a twinkle in the wise old eyes. 'In fact, I once did very much the same thing as you're doing now.'

'What, sir, you ran away?'

'That's right.' Mr Sampson cleared his throat. 'As a matter of fact I ran quite a long way before coming back.'

'Coming back?' repeated Johnny uncertainly.

Mr Sampson put an arm quietly around his rather thin, youthful shoulders.

'Oh, yes. You'll find the same, I expect. In the end one has to come back. Really, there's nothing much else for it. In fact, I rather fancy it's like that, you know, with things one runs away from.'

'Is it?'

Mr Sampson sighed, whether for Johnny's sake or his own it would be hard to say.

'I'm afraid it is.' He paused and looked around. 'Now look, I wonder if you might get out of here the way you came in, eh? And meet me outside. Will you promise?'

'All right,' said Johnny. 'Sir,' he added, almost shyly.

Outside the station Johnny felt quite glad to see the reassuring figure of Mr Sampson looming up. All at once the darkness and silence had seemed to gather around him, and somehow the idea of a trip to London didn't seem quite as romantic as it had done before.

'Well, now,' said Mr Sampson, putting a fatherly arm once more around the new boy's shoulders. 'Shall we take a little walk back to school now?

'And when we get back,' he went on, 'perhaps you'd like to join me with a cup of cocoa? My wife usually leaves one for me when I've been out late. I'm sure she wouldn't mind if we shared it together.'

He smiled: being really a very young old man.

'Just as I suggest that in the circumstances, you know, we might be well advised to, er, share this little escapade, eh, boy?'

The next morning Johnny got up and went to breakfast as usual. There was no stir, no commotion, no dramatic newspaper headlines. But at breakfast he did catch Mr Sampson's eye, and the housemaster quite definitely and emphatically winked.

Somehow that wink made Johnny feel at home for the first time. He began to think that maybe school wasn't going to be all that bad, after all.

III

The White Car

The white car used to pass through our village regularly. Some folks tried to make out it had been coming and going for a long time, but this I rather doubt. It just suddenly seemed to exist, a daily feature of our lives.

It was a beautiful car. I can't exactly remember the make, but it was one of those older, more solid, altogether more individual cars. The name doesn't matter, anyway: enough to say that it was a thing of beauty and a joy to behold as it sped sleekly down the long hill, across the wide village square and then out again into open country.

Usually the white car passed through some time in the afternoon, so that in a way we almost knew when to expect it – yet somehow we were never quite prepared. There was something almost ghostly about the swiftness and comparative silence of its journey: no sooner had it loomed like some mysterious ship on the horizon than with a sigh and a whisper it had travelled past in a slithering glistening of white light ... Yes, I must say the effect was rather disturbing, even a little sinister. Where did it come from? Where was it heading? Why did we never see it make the return journey?

It was when we combined to share our attempts at identification that we found the matter even more puzzling. For though there were plenty of us in the village who had seen the white car it soon emerged that nobody else had ever shared this experience. The farmer who lived a mile before the village, for instance – he had never seen the car go by, never indeed.

But we had, all right, of that there could be no denying. There wasn't one of us living in that village who hadn't some time or another heard the faint, unmistakable whine of the high-powered engine – who hadn't leaned out of a window just in time to see the white shape gliding past. Mr Curnow, the butcher, had seen it – so had Mr Hocking, the grocer, and Mr Andrewartha, the baker – so had Miss Parsons, the school teacher, and Mr Richards, the postman, and Mrs Jenkins, at the sweet shop.

So had I and a dozen others – and so, especially, had young Tilly Pascoe, the only daughter of the village postmistress. Tilly was rather a sad case, something of a worry to us all – a young girl with all a young girl's yearnings for love and friendship – but doomed to disappointment by a hare-lip and a face that was somehow almost painfully ugly. She was only too conscious of her defects and kept very much to herself, shut up in her mother's house. It had always seemed that nothing would tempt her out of this secretive way of life ... but in some way, the white car did. Whenever the sound of its approach was to be heard there would be a stirring in the house opposite us and I would see that familiar, ugly face pressed against the windowpane, staring out with strange eagerness. And somehow, more than once, I was struck by a fact – that at such moments Tilly looked so excited and intrigued that she became, well, almost pretty.

The white car ... its mysterious, shadowy outline seemed gradually to dominate our thoughts. It wasn't just the car, of course: it was the driver, too. Nobody had ever really seen the driver any more clearly than the car – after all it was always travelling at quite a speed. But we had all formed our impressions of a dark blob of a human being crouched low over the wheel in the open cockpit. As befitted such a vintage model, the driver wore a peaked cap and a scarf around the neck, and what with these and the turned-up neck of a leather jacket it would have been difficult to describe the features, even if there had been time to study them. Sometimes we exchanged opinions among ourselves but we never seemed to agree. Mrs Jenkins thought it was a fair young man with a moustache. Mr Curnow thought quite differently – it was, he said firmly, a middle-aged man with bushy eyebrows. Mr Andrewartha, on the other hand, thought it was someone even older, an old white-haired gentleman ... while Miss Parsons didn't think it was a man, but a wizened old lady, perhaps a witch.

And Tilly – what did she think? It used to puzzle me, because in some way I felt instinctively that she might have the right answer. Perhaps because of her disfiguration and ensuring life of withdrawal she always gave an impression of being not quite as other people ... almost of another world altogether. Such a person, I guess, might well know more about the strange white car than any of us.

Once I even tried to ask the girl, but she shut up like a clam. It was only from her frail, worried mother that I gathered that Tilly was indeed quite fascinated by the white car: looked on it almost worshipfully, yearningly, as one might on a knight of old. She waited for the car, one gathered, with bated breath and beating heart.

And so it went on, becoming an increasingly dominant part of our daily experience: the distant whine of the engine sounding a warning note that would make us pause in whatever we might be doing – then the ghostly white gliding apparition – and finally the lonely silence afterwards, in which, disturbed, we would take up our lives again.

At least the rest of us would – of Tilly, I was not so sure. Ever since the white car had made its first appearance Tilly had seemed to be a changing person – indeed, perhaps even a changeling. Living in the house opposite, as I did, I could not help noticing the signs – and especially the way in which the plain, ugly girl would seem for a moment to blossom and bloom at the arrival each day of the mysterious stranger in the white car.

'You'd almost think,' Tilly's mother confided one day, 'my girl do be proper hypnotised by that car.'

And indeed I began to think, so you might. For there could

be no doubt that gradually the fact of the white car passing through our village had become the most important single event in young Tilly's life. You might have said that she spent all the first part of the day looking forward eagerly to its appearance – and all the rest of the day bemoaning its disappearance. And along with that, so she waxed and she waned – one moment aglow with secret life, the next glum and despondent, uglier than ever.

And still, day after day, the white car zoomed along, swishing through the air, its big ribbed tyres hissing over the ground, its long graceful form curving across the wide streets. Day after day after day ... and always, somehow, conveying a curious air of intention, of ultimate purpose.

How would it all end? Somehow there was never any doubt in my mind – nor, I discovered later, among many other villagers – that it would end as abruptly as it began. But I suppose none of us could have been expected to guess just how ...

It was towards the end of the month, and at the time of the full moon, when we began to notice a strangeness about young Tilly – a kind of uneasy restlessness quite beyond her normal behaviour. Time and again I would look across and see her face pressed against the windowpane looking out as if in search of the white car, even when it was not likely to come – still she watched and watched, as if suddenly it had become more important than ever before that she should see it.

And then one day, one extraordinary day, the white car did not appear at its usual time. This was such a strange event that we all of us noticed and commented. Indeed, after a while, we began standing around in small groups, discussing the strange fact. And as time passed, and still there was no white car, we looked at one another uneasily.

Tilly Pascoe, in particular, was very disturbed. I caught glimpses of her in the house opposite, walking up and down and clasping her hands together, as if beset by a turmoil of emotions. Every time there was the sound of a car engine in the distance she would rush to the window and peer out hopefully ... only for her look of anticipation to fade into disappointment as some ordinary, humdrum vehicle went by.

Four o'clock, five o'clock, six o'clock, seven o'clock ... I think we had all of us begun to give up thoughts of the white car by then. It was dusk, too, a strange twilight hour when everything acquired an air of mystery and foreboding.

And then, far in the distance, we heard it – the familiar faint whine of the white car, coming down the long hill towards the village. Looking up and out into the duskiness it was just possible to make out the faint white speck, at first tiny on the horizon, then looming larger and larger.

It is difficult now, in the comfort of retrospect, to recapture the heightened atmosphere. Perhaps in some way we were all overwrought, and perhaps this has coloured our memories. But it did seem to me, and to the others, that on this occasion there was an unusually mesmeric effect about the approach of the white car through the gathering dusk. It was almost as if, more than ever before, it had a deliberate sense of purpose.

And that was the time when, as the white car zoomed down and down, nearer and nearer, the door of the house opposite was flung open and before any of us could make a move to stop her Tilly Pascoe came running out into the road. Perhaps she was caught up in some crazy mood, perhaps she was really hypnotized by the approaching white car – perhaps it was even more strange than that, and she was responding to some deep and primitive call ... I don't know, I really don't know.

I only know that, all in the confusion of a few moments, the white car loomed larger and larger, until its snarling, zooming, presence was there all around us – and at the same time the slip of a girl called Tilly Pascoe ran with arms outstretched as if in greeting – right into the path of the white car.

It was all over in a matter of seconds ... yet I still have this curious vivid recollection of the white car and Tilly seeming not so much to meet, but to merge, almost to become for a moment a single being ...

Then the white car had zoomed on, not stopping for a moment, roaring away into the distance ... and the still form of Tilly Pascoe was left crumpled in the roadway.

She was dead, quite dead, of course. But the strange thing was that on her face was a curious smile, lending her a kind of dignity in death – a smile almost as of recognition. As if – yes, I could not help thinking – as if in some weird way she had at last reached the driver of the white car, had perhaps finally recognised him for who he was ... the most important person in her life and death.

After that none of us was very much surprised to find that the white car never came back down the hill and through the broad street of our village ... never from that day to this.

IV

What's In A Name

When Jess and I decided to get married, we had one or two strictly practical aims and objects and high among them, Mary Jane.

'I've always wanted a beautiful baby girl,' said Jess dreamily. 'One with blue eyes and golden hair and a sort of Alice-in-Wonderland look.'

'That suits me fine,' I said.

'I can just see her now,' went on Jess. 'I've tied a blue ribbon in her hair and she's holding your hand and the pair of you are running down to the sea ...'

Well, I mean, who can resist an image like that? I was only too happy to fall in with Jess's wishes. Yes, it would be nice to have a pretty little girl and Mary Jane was a name I liked well enough. It had a flavour about it that helped to conjure up the kind of child I was sure we'd both adore.

It wasn't that we were a particularly soppy couple who thought for one moment that marriage was no more than a by-product of parenthood. Marriage should be fun, marriage should be magic – we intended it to be all these and we tried to prepare ourselves. We rambled bluebell woods hand-in-hand; we sat in smoky cafes discussing life and love; we climbed mountains just for the heck of it; we danced the clock round; we went on unconventional holidays across seas to new and exciting countries whose bright colours epitomised the new life ahead of us.

But at the same time we kept a small practical streak tucked away somewhere and we opened a special savings account at the post office with every now and then a ceremonial paying-in.

'For Mary Jane,' Jess would say, a mischievous gleam in her eyes.

'For Mary Jane,' I would echo.

That's what I mean when I say we had this feeling of having waited for Mary Jane a long, long time. In some strange way she was always there in the back of our minds, hovering on the fringe of our thoughts, colouring our future plans. She seemed a real, almost forceful personality.

Mind you, she had to take something of a back-seat at the time of our wedding. By that time Jess and I had passed through the usual hazards of love at first sight followed by hate at second sight, followed by renewed love, followed by — and so on and so on. I didn't approve of her high rate of smoking, she didn't like my passion for fast driving. Both of us were swift to go green-eyed if the other caught an admiring glance from members of the other sex and all the time, underneath all these surface dramas, some relentless old spider was spinning the web of love faster and faster.

By the time of our wedding day it had us firmly entangled. What's more, I fancy that we almost forgot Mary Jane during those early months when we got married and went off for a heavenly honeymoon and then returned to reality and took our dutiful place in two rented rooms in a quiet back street. They weren't much, those rooms, but when we'd stacked in our old belongings, somehow they began to seem like home.

By then again you might say, well — if we had forgotten Mary Jane, she had by no means forgotten us. I came home from work one day to find Jess sitting by the window in an unfamiliar pose of relaxation with her feet up.

'What's this?' I asked. 'Cook on strike? What about dinner? I'm starving.'

Jess hardly seemed to pay any attention. She looked dreamily out of the window.

'I really don't know whether I'll be allowed to cook you any more meals.'

'Why on earth not?' I said, trying to keep the irritation out of my voice.

Jess turned and for almost the first time in our married life, her gaze was indifferent.

'We're going to have a visitor.'

For a few moments she even let me fret about such an impending disaster. What troublesome relative or friend was it this time? Then she relented.

'It's all right – only Mary Jane.'

'Mary Jane?' I said and then a moment later. '*Mary Jane*!'

Then I picked Jess up and whirled her round and round in celebration and so we began, really began, waiting for Mary Jane.

At first I alternated between antagonistic unbelief that anything was happening – and frantic involvement with all the catastrophic possibilities. Jess, on the other hand, seemed to me increasingly casual about the whole business. Indeed, I began to feel it my duty to take her to task.

'I've been to the library and got a few books on motherhood. Maybe you'd like to read them?'

Jess yawned.

'Oh, I can't be bothered. Nature will have her way. Did you remember to get some oranges? I've a craving for oranges.'

'Don't you think you're eating too many oranges? I've been reading a most interesting book by a Dr Symovitch and not only is he against eating too much acid fruit, but he also wouldn't approve of the way you're sitting. Do you realise you might give the baby a morbidity complex?'

'Do be quiet. I want to rest.'

'Ah!' I exclaimed triumphantly. 'That's another book I've been browsing in. *Motherhood for Millions* and there it says it's all wrong for mother-to-be to remain too static. Restlessness is a virtue. A stationary mother is a bad mother ...'

That's when Jess threw an orange at me. Fortunately I ducked, but the orange hit a precious china ornament and smashed it into tiny pieces, whereupon – somewhat irrationally, I felt – Jess burst into a flood of tears and I had to spend half-an-hour comforting her.

But in general she remained impressively placid. In fact it was I who developed trends towards high blood pressure and general neurosis. I used to ring up four or five times a day from the office. In the end they got a bit shirty about it and I had to go out to the public telephone box, which made things a little expensive.

'What on earth's the matter with you?' asked my boss one day. 'You seem to be going to pieces. Haven't you got your mind on your work?'

I explained the simple, world-shattering fact.

'So what? Millions of women have babies.'

I looked superior.

'Ah, yes, but this one's different.'

I decided after that it was time to make some effort – especially after spending a depressing evening working out just what Mary Jane's arrival was going to involve. In fact, I began working overtime.

The boss seemed pleased about this. In fact, after a month or two he told me there was a chance of promotion, opening a branch up north.

I looked at him in horror.

'Oh, I couldn't think of moving just now. You see, Mary Jane's due in a few weeks and we've just done up the box room as a nursery and then Jess's got a friend who's coming in to help and after that ...'

My boss held up his hand wearily.

'All right, all right. I know. We mustn't forget Mary Jane.'

As the great day drew nearer it became impossible to forget Mary Jane, or indeed to think of anything else. Jess's parents had showered presents on us, huge parcels of nappies, crinkly bundles of baby clothes, a bath and other requisites. Not to be outdone, my own parents had come along and almost duplicated everything. Then, as word spread round, various uncles and aunts began to enter the fray, not always in the most tactful manner. Family feuds began to be rekindled.

More than once the sparks blew our way and Jess and I would glare angrily at one another.

'Why don't you tell your relatives to ...'

'And the same to yours!'

It was following one such acrimonious exchange, after we had retired to bed in sulky silence, and I was just uneasily dropping off, that Jess nudged me.

'Shh! I think it's started.'

Instead of following the good advice of shushing, I felt bound to institute some inquiries.

'Are you sure? Maybe it's just the baby kicking? What if it's just wind? Do you feel faint? Wait a minute. I'll just look up what Dr Symovitch has to say – '

'Ouch!' cried Jess. 'For goodness sake ring the doctor, will you?'

The next hour or so was the kind of personal nightmare, no doubt familiar to a few million husbands. A telephone out of order, a doctor on another case, a midwife on holiday, another doctor grumpily aroused – and in the end the arrival of a formidable ambulance and bustling attendants.

My last sight of Jess was somewhat depressing, being borne off on a stretcher, but she managed between spasms to wave to me and call out.

'It won't be long now – waiting for Mary Jane, I mean.'

In fact, it seemed rather like an eternity. I walked several miles round and round the hospital waiting-room and later, after they had turned me out for a while, round the neighbouring streets. Finally, as dawn broke, I went back timidly and stood cooling my heels for another hour or so.

At last, quite casually, one of the nurses passed by and responded to my agonised look.

'Oh, yes – would you like to see your wife? She's fine – the baby too!'

I fancy I was almost trembling as they guided me up to the ward. After all, I had waited a long time for this moment. I suppose I ought to have been remembering, in the best romantic style, all those highlights of our times together, the day we met, the day we mutually proposed, the wedding, but to tell the truth, I did none of these things. I just peered frantically up and down the ward until my eyes came to rest on Jess sitting up in bed, her face pale and tired, but wreathed in a welcoming smile.

As she saw me, she held her arms out and there was nothing in the world that mattered but to run forward and take her in my arms.

Then and only then, did I remember Mary Jane.

'The baby?'

I looked at Jess. There was something a little strange about her expression.

'She's not ...?'

'No, of course not.' Jess bent sideways and revealed a tiny unidentifiable bundle at her side. With a new, lovable air of ownership she lifted up the tiny lump of humanity and held it out towards me.

'Er, there is just one thing ...' Somehow Jess did not quite meet my eye. 'I don't think we can use the names Mary Jane after all.'

'But darling,' I began vehemently, 'you know we agreed – '

'Yes,' interrupted Jess sweetly, 'but really you know – it's not a very good name for a boy, is it?'

V

I Love You, Too, John

The girl was young and pretty. Dressed in blue jeans, black leather boots and a floppy grey sweater, she was like so many of her generation.

She stood on a corner of the busy street looking like the art student she was, yet somehow conveying, on closer inspection, a sense of disturbance, an air of suppressed despair.

When at last she crossed the road, she began counting the numbers on the houses and comparing them with a figure written on a slip of paper in her hand.

At last, finding the house she wanted, she went through a small iron gate and up to a massive black doorway. There was a small brass nameplate at one side and a bell above.

After hesitating a moment, the girl stretched out one finger and pressed.

The door was opened by a woman in a white coat. 'Yes?'

'I have an appointment with the doctor, but I'm a little early, I think.'

Nodding, the receptionist beckoned the girl in and showed her to a small waiting-room. The girl was relieved to find herself alone.

Suddenly weary, she leaned back in the chair, letting her dark head rest against the wall, staring up at the ceiling.

For the first time for many hours, she allowed herself to relax; and almost inevitably, she felt the tears welling up. She blinked violently to stop the impending waterfall. She couldn't cry – not just now.

But a few minutes later, seated in the leather-covered luxury of the doctor's consulting-room, she could stem the flow no longer.

'I'm sorry. I didn't mean to — '

'That's all right, my dear. I quite understand.'

The doctor patted her comfortingly on the shoulder. He was a rotund, cheerful little man, capable looking, kindly.

After a decent interval he passed over a packet of tissues.

When she'd dried her eyes, he began, 'Now perhaps you could answer one or two questions. Are you married?'

'Yes.'

'For how long?'

'Not long. A year, nearly.'

'I see. And who sent you to me?'

The girl, still trying to compose herself, gave the name of the friend who had sent her.

The doctor nodded, making a note, and then looked up. 'Well, before we go any further, I must know if you're sure about what you're doing. I mean, we mustn't pretend it's going to be an easy matter, must we? I'm prepared to help you if you've really decided there's no other way.'

The girl answered, her voice unnaturally strident for one so young and fresh-looking. 'No,' she said doggedly. 'There's no other way.'

His examination was swiftly professional.

'About three months pregnant,' he said carefully. 'So, in the circumstances, we won't waste time. I'd like you to come here tomorrow ...' The doctor's voice droned on, methodically outlining the procedures to be adopted. And it seemed to follow her out of the surgery. Even half an hour later, when she turned to enter her home, she could still hear the faint echo of that metallic, clipped voice telling her, 'Now, don't worry too much. It'll all be over in forty-eight hours.'

She let herself into the flat, glad of its emptiness. She didn't feel like talking to anyone at the moment, not even her husband.

Later that evening they sat facing one another in a curious

state of isolation by the small gas fire. He, too, was a student, now in his last year, studying history and philosophy; clever and sensitive, some of his ability reflected in the pale, strangely-handsome profile. He was well thought of at the college, she knew, and had a promising future; but now she could only think of him as the father of the baby she did not want.

He looked at her humbly, obviously ill at ease. 'You saw the doctor, then?'

'Yes.'

'He's willing to do it?'

'Yes. Tomorrow.'

Suddenly, irrationally, she longed to be able to throw herself into the comfort of his arms. But somehow there was a new, unfamiliar constriction between them.

'I'll get the money, then,' he said stiffly.

She nodded vaguely.

He looked at her, unhappiness set in his face. 'I'm sorry.'

'I expect you are – now,' she said bitterly.

'What about tomorrow, then?' he said after a while. 'I'd better come along, hadn't I?'

She shrugged. 'I suppose so. After all, it's your problem, too.'

That was what was so unfair, she felt later, tossing and turning, unable to sleep. The problem seemed to be hers alone. John had been kind and considerate, but, by his very diffidence and nervous anxiety to fit in with her wishes, he unconsciously increased her own burden. And what a terrible burden it was ...

In the still of the night, the girl let a tiny, heartfelt groan slip between her lips as she thought of what she was doing.

But what else could she do? They had both talked it over for hour after hour, both agreed it was the only sane and logical thing to do, rather than to jeopardise two college careers.

Yes, she reflected for the hundredth time, it was the sensible, practical thing to do.

At last, just as dawn was breaking over the surrounding

rooftops, the girl made up her mind. Or rather, unmade it. She couldn't go on with it – she just couldn't. She would never forgive herself.

She slept fitfully and when she awoke, instead of the familiar morning sickness which she had come to expect, she just felt wretched and miserable, uncomfortably aware of a strange, dull ache spreading over her body.

Somehow she forced herself to get up and go to college. On the way, she went into a telephone booth and rang up the doctor to explain her decision.

It was as she left the booth she had to hold on to the door for a few moments before it passed.

When she reached college she felt so ill she couldn't face the lecture. Instead, she sat in the common room.

A fellow student of John's passed by, and she asked him if he would fetch John.

She was sitting back in the chair, pale as a ghost, already gripped by pain, when John arrived. She saw the look of consternation on his face, and for a moment she was strangely touched.

Then she grabbed his arm urgently. 'Take me home, John. Please.'

To her surprise, John became enormously efficient. He borrowed a friend's car, helped her carefully into the passenger seat, and then speedily drove her home.

He helped her up the stairs and over to her bed, making sure she was relatively comfortable, before rushing off to fetch her doctor. Within twenty minutes they had returned.

The doctor's examination was brief. 'Well, young lady,' he said quickly, 'I think the best place for you is a hospital.'

She looked at him uncertainly, wincing between pains. 'Doctor, is it – '

He nodded. 'Yes, I'm afraid it looks like the beginning of a miscarriage. Of course, they'll do all they can to save the baby, but there's not much chance.'

It was really too ironic for words. She wanted to laugh and cry at the same time. But the tears won. They came flooding out, and she curled up, obsessed by the twin demands of pain and tears, tears and pain.

John knelt on the floor beside her, his arm around her shoulder.

'It'll be all right – don't cry. Everything will be all right.'

She looked at him through the mist of her own tears, and was moved to see the pain and suffering in his own eyes.

Forcing a tremulous smile, she reached out and put a hand up to his face. 'Don't cry, John,' she whispered rather sadly. 'Don't cry.'

'John,' she whispered much later, after the pain and the suffering were over and done with, leaving her feeling drained of all feeling and hope.

She was lying in the hospital ward now, and he was sitting beside her. She found it curiously youthful and appealing the way he leaned forward as if to hide their conversation from all the other possible watching eyes.

He took her hand in his own, as if feeling the need for contact.

'I'm sorry, John,' she whispered.

She felt him squeeze her hand, hard, unbearably hard, as if in some way he wanted to hurt himself through her.

'I'm sorry, too.'

She forced a faint, tremulous smile. 'At least it wasn't anything we did. At least I didn't – '

Slowly, and then more eagerly as he saw the relief it brought her, he nodded. 'No.'

She shook her head weakly. 'I'd have felt terrible, absolutely terrible. The doctors say it was probably all the worrying, that had something to do with losing the baby.'

He patted her hand gently. 'Yes, I expect it was.'

The girl turned her head away, looking across the long ward without seeing the other people, the other lives; only contemplating her own.

Her eyes filled with tears again. 'I've made such a mess of things.'

'No, you haven't,' he said indignantly. 'We have.'

The girl turned her head and smiled faintly. 'You've been

wonderful. Aren't you fed up? Wouldn't you like to go?'

He shook his head violently. 'No, I don't want to go. I'll stay until ...'

Until what, she wondered. Until this heavy feeling leaves me? Until my body gets over its terrible shock? Until ...?

And then, suddenly, John bent forward over the hospital bed, one hand gently touching her hair, brushing it back, his eyes burning into hers with a strange intensity more electrifying than any previous look they had given her. And a voice that somehow was deeper and older than it had sounded before, was murmuring into her ear, shyly, tenderly, 'I love you ... I did before, but now it seems much more. It's just that somehow ...'

The boy's eyes crinkled up helplessly, and he smiled, uttering simply, but with strange conviction, again and again, 'I love you ... I love you ...'

The girl who had been young and pretty and dressed in the brightly casual manner of many of her generation, but now lay tired, wan, and quite exposed on her hospital bed, felt somehow deep, deep down inside of her a tiny new spark of life being kindled.

Looking up into the familiar eyes of the man she was beginning to know and love for the first time, she had the strangest, wildest, most exciting intimations of their new future together, of something real and wonderful being built that might never before have existed.

But too tired now for words, she just smiled faintly and murmured, 'I love you, too, John.'

Then she fell asleep, her hand lying trustingly in his.

VI

Grass In Winter

Grass in winter clings to the feet with the hungry grasp of the unloved, cold and lifeless to the touch. The grass is lean and coarsened by the wind, dulled by sunless rains. Bare to the frowning sky, it bends and sways tremulously across lonely landscapes, occasionally shuddering as if from some deep, unknown agony of frustration. Like a vast sea, empty of purpose, grass in winter is alone and friendless, its reality of warmth and colour drained deep into the sleeping earth.

In a field of thick, dark grass the soldier from another country crouched while the early but hidden sun struggled to colour the clouds. He crouched low in the grass, forgetting where he had come from, losing his other world into the coarse unreality of his new world. Around him the grass arose disinterestedly, high enough to shelter him from curious eyes, high enough to wash his dull uniform with a cold green sea.

Hidden in the grass, the soldier breathed uncomfortably, constantly brushing the hard stalks out of his face. He had taken off his helmet and strapped it to his haversack, to avoid any danger of light being reflected from its surface. Now his hair, wet and dank from the morning dew, hung matted across his forehead, shrouding his small, square-set face. He looked tired and sleepless ... the darkness of his expression was emphasised by a straggly stubble of beard. Only the eyes bespoke life, darting from side to side nervously – wide green pinpoints among the wild green grass. The eyes burned with anxious life, while his tongue ran thick and dry, and a spasmodic sick feeling caught at his stomach.

Cautiously, for the first time since the light had come, the soldier moved. Slowly he raised his dark, rain-soaked head until it floated silently among the thin tops of the grass, like a dead log drifting in a lake. His eyes peeped at the long bent rows of grass, watched the shallow blends of green disappearing down the hillside ... saw, uneasily, the faraway hedges, the grey-blue tint of a farm cottage. Slanting sideways, as the dead log aimlessly slants, the soldier's eyes followed another slope of green, endless across desolate fields, burying on the horizon in the faint glint of a river. Turning, and looking behind, he saw again only the wide sheet of his own field, curving suddenly to meet the sky, falling into some eternity beyond his gaze.

The soldier shivered. He fingered nervously at the cold wet shaft of his rifle, stretched beside him in the grass. His mind flickered irritably, longed to flash away beyond the horizon. Only with difficulty could he bring himself to concentrate on the reality of this world of cold green grass to which he now belonged utterly. Except that he was lost, he knew nothing. He did not know whether the dull rumble of guns on the horizon were made by the enemy or his own side – whether the roar of sudden battle that had swept him along on its tide the previous day had ebbed away into nothingness, or stormed on to new horizons ... or merely sunk into the very fields, to bubble like a volcano awaiting the next spurt. He was only aware, instinctively, of a scent of death in the passing wind, wafted from some hidden, unrealised centres of life among the innocent waves of grass that filled his view. And he hated the long, treacherous grass, hated its evil secretiveness, even as he knew that his safety depended on it ... He remembered how, in summer, the grass at home would be thick and warm and soft, so that he could sink into its folds and float into dreams. Now the grass had no warmth, no softness: it was only unreal – strands of shadowy, dank unreality. He could feel the long stalks, but they were cold and dead, and when he sank among them they parted lifelessly.

Most of the night he had lain curled uncomfortably on the hardened soil. Thick as his uniform was, he had felt the cold and the wetness gradually seeping through, until the clothes were damp and clogging, chilling into his skin, paining his bones. The breaths he took were heavy with wetness from the grass, and hurt his lungs. He was thankful when the grey light had come. He felt that if he had lain there much longer he would have frozen into the cold earth.

When the morning had fully risen, the soldier began to crawl slowly through the grass. He crawled on his belly, for in parts the grass fell short and he dared not take any risks of being seen. He crawled like a snake, wriggling slowly and stealthily through some green, overhanging undergrowth. It struck him, in fact, that the grass itself was composed of so many snakes – dying snakes that wound and coiled around him as he crawled. Viciously he smashed ahead of him with the butt of his rifle, breaking and tearing the surprised stalks. It gave him a sense of pleasure, almost of power, to do this. It relieved a strange buried fear within him.

After a time, the soldier came to the end of the field and climbed through a hedge into the next field. He was moving in the direction of the plains where he felt vaguely there was more chance of discovering his whereabouts. Soon he came to the outskirts of the small cottage he had seen. Here the grass petered out into a muddy garden, and he was forced to remain some distance away, pressed deep into the grass for a desperate shield. He lay there for some time and was thankful for his caution as, with a thud at his heart, he saw a man emerge from the back of the cottage. He recognised the enemy uniform. For a moment his finger itched at the trigger of his gun; then he let go, frightenedly, hearing other voices from within the kitchen ... Two other men came to the doorway.

The wave of fear that came over him tingled at his skin, shivering into his hair. He lay nerveless on the dead grass, conscious of the flimsiness of the stalks, fearful that a gust of wind would suddenly blow them aside. Only after what seemed an eternity, when the men had gone in again, did he stir. Then he began backing away into deeper grass, making a wide circuit of the cottage as he passed on down the slope. But after he had disappeared, one of the men came out into the garden again and, looking casually out to the field, caught sight of the pathway forced through the grass. He hurried towards this, his look of curiosity fading into sudden alarm.

By the middle of the day the soldier had crawled down the slope and on to the plain, but still he found himself deep among seas of clinging grass. As he crawled from one field to another it seemed to him that he was lost, queerly and for ever, in the endless waves of grass. Looking around him, he could see nothing else, no other signs of life – of roads or habitation. Only here and there, coming across half-hidden bodies of dead soldiers, was he reminded that death had passed this way before. Being reminded, he felt sickened again. He crouched lower in the grass, frightened of the oncoming clumps of green, suspicious of the distant breezing grass-tops at which he aimed.

He became aware of the hunger. It was more than twelve hours since he had eaten. With him he had only a water flask, already half empty; and some biscuits. He ate these slowly, savouring the dry taste to the full. Then he lay on his back, gazing up at the colourless sky. By closing his eyes he could shut himself off from the one world, and the other world surged joyously into his thoughts. Drowning into sleep he was still faintly aware of the soft wind blowing across the field. He felt, strangely, the harsh rub of the grass against his hands and under his head; and then he fell asleep.

When he awoke he was surprised to find a thin shaft of sunlight falling upon the green-sloped horizon. Fascinated, he followed it, watching it creep like a finger across the waving grass. The sunlight crept towards him, wavered, then broke around him, flooding the field with whiteness. But even as he felt the unexpected warmness on his cheeks he sensed an intrinsic falsity about it. It was not the warmth he had felt at home in the summer fields, it was a false warmth, a false sun, giving out dead sunshine to the dead grass. He ran his fingers through the grass beside him: it was unchanged – dank, cold, lifeless, unawakened by the sunshine. He tore up the unresisting stalks, throwing them away in sudden revulsion.

When next he moved, it was with a strange urgency. He was suddenly conscious of the endless evil lurking in the grassy, bland-faced fields. He shuddered at the thought of the shallowness, the bareness, the inadequacy of the grass. He longed to rise to his full height and take deep grateful gulps of the sweet fresh air, free from the harsh smell of the soil, the damp odour of the grass. Yet even as the longing grew on him, tormenting him, tantalising him, he felt the necessity to crouch even lower, to drag himself even more quickly through the slithering wet grass. His eyes ached from endless peering through the waving tree-tops of grass. His cheeks smarted from the cuts of the coarse grass stalks. Sometimes a tuft of grass choked his nostrils, sticking to his mouth, leaving an unpleasant taste on his tongue as he spat it out.

He crawled on, across the longest and most tortuous of all the fields. It seemed to stretch half-way across the plain. Looking sideways, he could see, far away, the field from where he had started, and the innocent blue tiles of the cottage. But his eyes blinked from the effort of looking, and he turned and went forward. He crawled on and on and on ... and as he did so it seemed to him that the grass deepened and grew thicker, rising higher and higher, engulfing him so that he could hardly breathe or open his mouth or his eyes. And with it he felt a terrible unknown fear burning within him, a sensation of wanting suddenly to hide from something, like the worm fearful of the hovering bird wings.

He pressed himself deeper into the grass, but as he did so it seemed to cling thicker and tighter to his body, winding around him, clutching at his throat, grasping at his thick boots, dragging him down into its cold, empty arms. The wetness of the grass, the endless cold wet kiss of the grass on his skin sent tremors through his body ... He felt like a drowning man, burrowing forward desperately into the thickening walls of grass – only to feel himself being overwhelmed, feeling the grass mounting round him like the sea waves. It seemed that the grass was holding him, dragging him down, wrapping one long tentacle after another around his limbs so that he was relentlessly borne down and halted. He felt himself drowning in the grass, felt his other warm, loving worlds slipping and fading away: while around him ominous menacing shadows fell across the cold sunlight ...

Crying out in anguish, he suddenly scrambled to his feet. His eyes, round and fearful, stared desperately at some unseen horizon. He began running, stumbling awkwardly as the grass clung heavily to his feet.

He did not hear the shots that rang out bleakly. He twisted round and fell, slowly and grotesquely, crumbling his outstretched shape into the thick grass.

The enemy men who had trailed him from their outpost cottage came up to him and went methodically through his pockets. When they had finished they turned and began tramping back.

Later, the sky darkened and a lonely wind blew across the vast quiet field, blowing the cold grass in green waves, hiding the soldier for ever.

VII

Castles In The Sand

When I was a small boy of ten I wore beach shorts and an old panama hat of my father's and spent day after day of the long summer holiday building sandcastles on the wide sandy beach at Llantyllan.

I usually left my mother sitting on the shingle and walked a long way out, trailing my bucket and spade across the sands, until I came to an isolated part where I felt I could be safe from possible interference by other children. Then I selected a smooth patch of sand and started cutting deep into it with the thin blade of my tin spade. First I dug a circular trench, throwing the sand into a heap in the middle, then I built the castle out of the piled-up sand. Using only the back of my spade I carefully shaped the square formidable outline of the castle, carving out turrets and high walls and a tower. Sometimes I collected handfuls of wet stones or pieces of wood and stuck them in various places along the castle top, to represent soldiers. Once, I remember, I found an old piece of lead piping, on my way down to the sands, and this served as a most impressive castle gun, protruding menacingly over one wall.

When the last artistic touch had been given to the castle I dug another trench, leading down to the sea. As soon as the oncoming waves began to penetrate into this, I ran back as fast as I could to my castle and took up a proud position within its sanctuary, crouching behind the towering walls

(they reached at least to my knees). From there I watched the
water surging towards me – pounding into the circular trench
and forming a natural moat around the castle – isolating me,
temporarily, into an exciting world of my own. I remember
how I used to remain there until the last possible moment –
until the sea made its final, overwhelming advance, over-
running the moat and crumbling the flimsy castle walls, and I
had to make a run for it, splashing and shouting across wet
stretches of sand towards the safety of higher land.

I liked being on my own because if I was with other children
I could not indulge in my own games of fantasy – they didn't
seem to be so much interested in building sandcastles as in
knocking them down, jumping and stamping on them until
they were flattened into the sands – and this used to make me
feel very frightened. One day, however, my mother came
hurrying across to me and said excitedly that there was to be a
competition to see which child could build the most beautiful
sandcastle, and I agreed to forsake my happy isolation. There
was to be a first prize of a brand-new bucket and spade and a
free seat at the local pierrot show but it was not this that
attracted me. What I could not resist was the challenge to a
tremendous vanity burning within me.

· We gathered on a wide stretch of dry sand, well away from
the white line of the sea. Altogether there were about twenty-
five children – some only tiny tots, most of them about my own
age – and around us a crowd of fluttering, laughing parents.
One of the park-keepers, a red-faced ex-sailor, came and gave
the starting signal, after telling us we would be allowed an
hour in which to build our sandcastles. 'One-two-three –
OFF!' he bawled, and everyone hoorayed, and then, most of
us looking rather self-conscious, we began digging.

At first there was much cheering and shouting, especially in
encouragement of the small children struggling manfully to
wield their spades without falling over. But interest gradually
languished, parents went back to their knitting and their
sunbathing, and after a time we were left more or less to
ourselves. I didn't bother about what the others were doing
but went to work as if I were on my own, only this time taking

greater care than ever. I felt very happy, partly because it was so warm and lovely out there, partly because I felt tremendous confidence in my prowess as a builder of sandcastles. It gave me a warm feeling, as I lovingly modelled and patted the outlines of my castle, to know that nobody else would build such a beautiful castle. With the quiet pride of the true artist I created my most ambitious castle – laboriously fashioning the tall, shapely walls, the delicate, curving turrets, the round firm lines of the tower.

It was only after about half an hour that I took a glance around me. Then I was surprised to see that many of the others had made very little progress. Several children had given up and gone away to play. Of those that remained, the only one who had progressed to any extent was my neighbour, a little girl of eight or nine in a short, light-blue dress, her hair tied in a great brown mop by a bright red ribbon. She had her face bent down as she worked, and her legs, browned a deep tan by the sun, stuck out of the ground like young sapling trees. She seemed to be taking it all very seriously. But, glancing over at her handiwork, I decided that it was cruder and less polished than my own.

No doubt some such doubt began troubling her, for after a while she began casting sidelong glances in my direction. Soon I noticed her straighten up and come walking over towards me, with a studied air of carelessness. She came and stood beside me without saying a word, watching as I carefully cut out the shapes of a turret along one side of my castle. At length I began to feel uncomfortable and stopped work, looking up at her inquiringly. She just looked at me out of round, surprised blue eyes, saying nothing – but something in the way she looked and something in the way her eyes were so round and innocent, yet so full of hidden meanings made me feel strangely uneasy. I felt, trembling and unexpressed, a slow wave of resentment surging out of her. I was glad when she turned away and went back to her castle. Watching the quiet business-like movements of her spade I was conscious only of wishing ever so much that I had never looked up and noticed her there, next to me.

Suddenly I heard her call out to me. I put down my spade and went over. She looked at me with her round eyes, and I could have sworn they were swimming with tears. She pointed to one side of her castle, to where part of a wall had broken in, and said falteringly that she couldn't reach it properly. So I smiled with the clumsy graciousness of a boy of ten, and I carefully got down on my knees and stretched over. It was a difficult task, and it took me two or three minutes to straighten out the wall.

When I got to my feet again she was standing just behind me. I turned and found her quite close to me, so close that her mass of tumbling brown hair tickled my cheek. I half averted my face, but I looked into her eyes and saw they were suddenly laughing and bright with life, and I couldn't help smiling back. We stood there close, looking at each other and smiling, and I felt a warmness I had never felt before.

Then I went back across the sands to my castle. I didn't really look until I was right back, and then I stopped abruptly, a heavy weight clamping me to the ground. My sandcastle lay in ruins, a crumpled mass of churned-up sand. I couldn't believe my eyes at first, I shut them and opened them again, but it was still there. The walls were mown down in great gashes, and the turrets and the dainty tower had vanished, and there was no shape – no shape at all about the ugly lumps of scattered sand.

I turned quickly and ran back to the little girl with the red ribbon in her hair. She was bending down, quietly getting on with the building of her castle. It was large and neat, and nearly completed – not a beautiful castle, but beautiful compared to what was left of mine.

I felt the hot tears springing up, felt the unnatural flush of my cheeks. I could hardly speak.

'Oh, you beast!' I cried. 'Oh, you-you-you beast! Beast! Beast. Beast! Beast!'

I stood there outraged and aflame, mad with a desire to run at the little girl and push her deep into the middle of her castle, to bring *her* world crumbling down about her. But she turned and looked at me out of her wide eyes, alive with the strangest tantalising light, and I could only stand there helplessly, howling and crying like I thought I would never do again – the tears pouring down my cheeks and splashing endlessly into the insatiable sands. They came and gave the little girl the first prize, and said what a clever girl she was and what a beautiful castle she had built.

I went away and sulked and cried to myself, and for a long time afterwards I was frightened to go near the sands for fear that the little girl would come up to me and look at me out of her round blue eyes, turning my life topsy-turvy.

VIII

The Model

The model was halfway through the session when the stranger came quietly into the studio and sat down in a far corner, took out his sketch-book and began drawing. There were already half a dozen students in the room as well as the rather languid, elderly art teacher, all of them predictably familiar to the model and no more disturbing than the wooden stools and easels. But the stranger in the corner was different; unfamiliar and unknown, somehow a silent threat to the ordered pattern of the morning.

The model did not betray her awareness of the situation by so much as the slightest change of expression or movement: not for nothing had she earned the reputation at the art school of being the most skilled of all the models, able to hold effortlessly a variety of poses of infinite grace, the epitome of utter stillness. She continued to stare into space with her face drained of outward expression, her eyes lost in some faraway dream, her body frozen into its curvaceous image and partially shrouded by long strands of black hair spilling around sensuous white shoulders. She looked every man's dream of pure and tranquil beauty: and yet, paradoxically, in the eyes of the students she was no more than an arithmetical mixture of lines and shadows.

Yet that was not the way the stranger saw her from his distant corner on the other side of the room: this the model knew out of a deep and disturbing instinct so that though not a flicker crossed her outward mask somewhere within her innermost being there stirred unwilling beginnings of a secret awareness. It was as if the proverbial pebble had dropped into the centre of a calm pool, sending its relentless ripples forever outwards, further and further, exposing every hidden crevice.

At first the model burned inwardly with a fierce indignation at such an unwarranted intrusion upon her sacred privacy. She was used to the nakedness of her flesh being revealed to all those staring eyes – such exposure meant even less to her than it did to the painters with their technical absorption. She had long ago learned the lesson which every woman learns at one stage or another and knew that she could be most private when least protected and that what these students saw, anyway, was only what she chose to reveal. The model herself, her inner nakedness, remained inviolate. She could, if she wished, be more alone in this room of a dozen people than by herself at home ... if she withdrew, consciously, then she was no longer there, it was as simple as that. This of course, as the art master appreciated, was what made her such an excellent model.

But it was not like that with the stranger in the corner. It was not like that from the moment the door opened and he appeared like a disturbing shadow from – where? Where had he come from? Why was he here? What could be the meaning of the fact that his mere presence hung like a dark cloud in a clear blue sky? Who was he, this stranger?

Because he had chosen to sit in the very furthest corner, immersed in the shadows of that area, at no time was the stranger clearly visible to the model – while at every moment she was visible to him in every detail. This fact, which normally never worried her in relation to the students, now began to gnaw at her secret perceptions, starting as no more than a tiny flame and then gradually burning brighter and brighter. At first, contemptuously, she told herself that she would not be intimidated and that with her mind she would banish this – after all – ill-defined and clumsily formulated threat. She would tell herself that there was no stranger in the corner staring across the abyss at her, that it was all no more than some hallucination of the lazy morning's boredom.

The trouble was, the model discovered to her chagrin, that while her mind sought to rule, her body insisted on obeying: while her mind attempted obliteration of the fact, her body secretly accepted, even welcomed the fantasy. Just as all her mental processes were rigorously concentrated on achieving total rejection – so at that very moment there arose a strange and unfamiliar warmth in the centre of her being, spreading out delicately to the very extremities of her limbs so that, gently but unmistakably, they tingled. Suddenly she realised that if she could have moved her head and looked downwards she would have seen a final evidence: slowly but with growing firmness the nipples of her breasts had come to secret life, were erect and tactile, almost as if responding to some secret caress ...

Despite herself, while maintaining her outward mask, subtly the model allowed her dreaming eyes to slant downwards so that they were no longer staring up through the large side windows at the mysteries of the cloud-driven sky outside – but instead looking more directly across the confinements of the room. She felt obsessed suddenly by the necessity to grapple more firmly with this unimaginable threat. Or was it a threat? How could such a pleasurable experience really be a threat? She banished such a weak and unworthy thought from her mind even as, without really moving, it seemed to her that her limbs trembled as if with secret physical delights, familiar from other more private times in her life but unknown, indeed unallowable, here on the public platform. No, she would not allow this intrusion. She would not, she would not ...

If only she could see the stranger – yes, that was it. If she could but see his face, his outline, his stranger's person, then perhaps the very mundane reality would reduce the curious sense of disturbance. Oh, if only she could see him! Across the room, unknown to the other students working away at their tasks, her blank eyes searched and searched. Was that his figure, outlined so vaguely against the shadows? Yes, surely that was the stranger, tall and slender, like the branch of a sturdy tree. She thought she caught glimpses of a slight movement, signs of a head bending forward ... but of course he, too, was drawing, drawing her, seeing her across all that distance, capturing her with his secret eyes and translating his vision to the virgin white paper of the sketch-book.

Suddenly the stranger looked up and for a brief moment it seemed to the model as if his eyes burned bright and fiercely out of the shadows as he looked carefully upon that which he sought to transcribe into his sketch-book. The eyes remained shadowy and uncertain to the woman's gaze and yet they were a hundred times brighter and more direct than any of the other casual watching eyes. She understood this not with her mind but, again, with her body, and she knew that when the stranger looked at her from the far corner of the room it was as if he stood at her side holding up a magnifying glass and that in the opaque enlargement of that glass he was somehow seeing not merely her outward linear form – but far beyond that, into her inner being, her secret soul.

This knowledge both alarmed and frightened the woman, and yet also enthralled her. She had never before encountered a gaze so piercing and relentless, and yet so exquisitely sensuous. Even though she had as yet seen no more than a distant shadowy figure, and now an uncertainly defined glance – already by instinct, and as she knew in her heart by preference, she was a captive. Not only was she the object of his searching, seeking gaze – but this was assuredly what she wanted, more devoutly than anything else in the world.

As she admitted this awareness to the furthermost corners of her being the woman felt her whole body awakening as if from some long sleep; a strange warmth diffusing through her veins so that she was no longer conscious, as often she would be at this stage of a session, of any kind of weariness. Instead she felt extraordinarily alive, fiercely so, and such was the strength and power of this feeling that she grew frightened. Surely something of this upheaval would be reflected on her outward face, in some movement of those immobilised limbs, perhaps in some sudden wild light in the soft liquid eyes?

But no: the students continued with their drawings, heads

bent down for the most part but whenever lifted showing no surprise, obviously seeing no more than the ever familiar figure of the model, holding one of her ever familiar poses. And seeing this, appreciating her continued freedom, the model felt a glorious sense of release to think that she was free to give herself up to the real and secret meaning of the moment. She slanted her eyes even more in the single direction so that she stared across at the stranger – and as she did so she had the distinct impression that for a magic moment a shaft of sunlight fell through the window and briefly illumined that distant shadowy corner. She saw, all at once, a more definite outline of the stranger; he became a dark and real being who, unlike her, wore clothes – yet before her gaze, perhaps by an effort of her will in fact, might well have been sitting there in the same glory of nakedness. She saw – sensed, surmised, *knew* – that within these shadows there lurked a beautiful being of shining skin and taut muscles and rippling movements, a truly godlike creature. Yes, she knew this must be so.

Not a word was said. At the end of the session while the students stirred and gathered together their things and prepared to depart the model unfolded her languid limbs and put on a silken gown and then walked purposefully across the room to where the stranger sat, still shrouded in the shadows. As she approached him he looked up with his stranger's smile and at the same time handed her the large white sketchbook in which, she saw at a glance, he had captured with a few strokes everything about her which was known only to herself, which none of the other students could possibly have known. She met the stranger's luminous eyes, unafraid, and gave a smile. Then she turned and walked quickly over to the dressing room, hastily throwing off the gown and then pausing for a thoughtful moment to look at her white and suddenly virginal body in the long gilt mirror. At last, growing impatient, she began putting on the temporary cloak of her everyday clothes.

When she came out and rejoined the stranger and he rose to his feet, it seemed to the model that he towered above her, a positive giant of a being, at once possessive of her spirit and being. With a curious smile in her direction he picked up his drawing and tore it into small shreds, throwing them high into the air so that they floated away in all directions, like confetti.

Then, with the model taking his arm and falling easily into step with him, the stranger walked out of the door again. As the two of them descended the steps outside and began walking away down the long, long road of their life together they seemed to merge into the same shadowy figure – and then vanish forever.

IX

Alien Beauty

The fact that the girl was coloured hardly seemed significant to Ashley – until too late. Indeed if anything there was a kind of lightness about her, an almost ethereal glistening shining quality, which drew him irresistibly at first. He often found himself comparing her to some precious stone that had been polished and polished, and now exuded a disturbing, secretive glow. Why, her very presence in the room caught the eye like some shaft of unexpected sunlight – or perhaps, more accurately, moonlight. For there was about her, unmistakably, a suggestion of the darker, more mysterious side of life.

The way in which they met was somehow symbolic of the whole unreal atmosphere of their relationship. Ashley's garrulous and self-centred old grandmother had, somewhat unreasonably in Ashley's opinion, attained her ninetieth birthday, and to celebrate this occasion a grand and rather daunting family reunion had been planned. This was being held up in Liverpool, one of those provincial cities which before the advent of the Beatles had been fixed in Ashley's Southerner's imagination as some kind of outpost of the frozen North. It was still hardly a place he would ever have willingly visited, from out of the comfortable tedium of his commuter life in Surrey, but then it had been his grandmother's home for some years past and it was difficult really to refuse the pressing invitation. And so he made the long and tedious journey up to the grimy dome of Lime Street Station ... there to be met by a woman in a large straw hat whom he vaguely remembered as Great-Aunt Maud, and whisked off to her ultra suburban house in Crosby. Finally, on the day of days – which could not come soon enough for Ashley – he was carried off in some triumph, rather like someone's pet trophy, to the great party.

This, Ashley was relieved to discover, was not being held at one of the various relatives' uniformly mediocre houses, nor even at his grandmother's more commodious but equally bourgeois villa on the edge of Speke Park – but in fact, surprisingly, at the Adelphi Hotel in the centre of Liverpool, one of those enormous gilt flavoured (and no doubt edged) edifices which for better or worse constitute the best that can be done by the British hotel industry. At least in what sometimes seemed to Ashley like marble halls of antiquity there was space and an opportunity to move around, so that as the guests gathered in alarming numbers it was still possible to avoid the awful claustrophobia which, Ashley felt sure, would have overcome him in someone's house or flat.

And then, just as he was steeling himself to go and do his stint of making polite conversation to the old lady, presiding like a queen at her court at the top of a long table, Ashley saw the girl. He wasn't looking anywhere in particular and then somehow his gaze was irresistibly drawn in one direction – and there she stood, quiet and cool and calm, and yet somehow, to him, shimmering with secret life.

He stood and stared for quite a long time ... perhaps in some way the very intensity of his gaze communicated over the distance, for all at once she half turned her head and looked across at him. He had the impression that fleetingly, almost doubtfully, she caught his stare, meeting it with a certain boldness, and then looked away again. At the end of that single moment he found himself trembling, shot through by a strange feeling such as he had not known for many years – if ever.

Later on he managed to circulate his way cautiously over towards the alcove where the girl stood engaged in animated conversation with several people – one of whom, Ashley was relieved to recognise as a distant cousin. He greeted her with unexpected warmth and at last, after some irritating small talk, was himself introduced to the girl whose ebony aspect suddenly dominated his vision.

Her name, it appeared, was Arlene, an unusual enough one to be true, and she was at the party because she ran a hair-dressing saloon frequented by various members of his grandmother's circle – in fact that very morning she had been responsible for setting the old lady's silver tresses. But none of this information really registered on Ashley, besides the impact of the girl herself: her whole, strangely vibrant being. He noticed that she was not only tall but quite large generally – but with a size of strengthness and virility, not of flabbiness. She had in fact, and it was disturbingly easy to observe, the kind of animal-like body which defied all attempts to clothe it in respectability: so that, though she wore a demure enough silk dress, this served as little more than a mere decor for the undulating and curvaceous qualities supposed to be hidden. And then from out of this generously physical body there rose up, with unexpected grace, a swan-like neck and a face and head of almost classical beauty; the cheek-bones high and striking, the mouth sensually wide, the eyes deep-set and full of tantalising shadows. In short, she was a girl of striking and unfamiliar attraction.

Or so it seemed to Ashley, on that hitherto cold and grey day inside the large lounges of the Adelphi Hotel, Liverpool. He could not get over the fortuity of the encounter, nor the continuing pleasure it gave – nor, indeed, the contemplation of what further pleasures might lie in store.

'You know,' he said when, after a while, by a combination of good fortune and judicious guidance, he had edged the girl away from the others, 'I had no idea Liverpool was blessed with someone like you.'

The girl laughed, a natural, easy-going laugh that revealed much of her character.

'I expect you'd soon find others if you troubled to look.'

'But why should I? – when there is you!'

The girl laughed again. He found himself almost as fascinated by her voice, low and husky and suggestive, as by her appearance.

'Tell me about yourself,' he said quickly. 'What are you doing – ' he made a desultory gesture ' – here?'

He supposed the girl appreciated the directness of approach; at any rate to his pleasure he found her paying him the compliment of giving him her whole attention for what really amounted to the rest of the party. They bandied words, her native intelligence more than matching his more sophisticated wit: once or twice her sharpness of observation impressed him greatly, and she also had a piquant turn of phrase ... and yet, all the time, no matter how rapidly he talked, he was aware of a different stream running deep down, an aching physical awareness of the girl. When she laughed and showed the brilliant whiteness of her teeth he was fascinated by the flashing symbol of something slightly alien and unknown. When she gave a sudden movement and stretched her graceful neck he could not take his eyes off the throbbing vein, a pulsating revelation of her whole being. In fact he was so engrossed with his private interpretation that he quite forgot to be his usually rather affected self and spoke with a certain natural warmth, which made quite an impression ...

So that when he said, tentatively, that it would be rather nice if they could meet again some time he was pleasantly surprised at the response.

'Yes, I would like that.'

'Well, then,' he said eagerly. 'When ... ?'

They met one misty afternoon when he had managed to escape from the clamouring family conferences: not quite knowing what else to do they went for a long rather aimless walk along the docks. It was cold and rather miserable, and after a while the girl shivered.

'Here, you mustn't get cold,' said Ashley, and he put a decisive, protective arm round the girl's shoulders. Even under the thick wool of her coat he could feel the warmth, as if what it was that made her so alive and vibrant and passionate flooded through everything. He walked along in the slightly uncomfortable position, the girl saying nothing, until at the end they came to a railway over-looking one of the ferry-boat landing stages. They watched one of the big squat boats manoeuvre in and disgorge its teeming hundreds of passengers and then, with frothing propellers, edge away into the murky river.

Suddenly Ashley gripped the girl's shoulder fiercely and pulled her round. He had time in the moment of eternity that ensued to see the girl's face illuminated by a nearby lamp, so that once again it seemed almost pale and phosphorescent – a background to dark eyes as bright as coals, nostrils quivering, thick lips half drawn back as if instinctively in preparation. The next moment he had placed his own mouth over hers and was kissing her with an insistent, demanding passion that surprised them both.

At the end of the embrace they were both a little shaken. Ashley recovered himself first.

'I must see you.' He made a gesture, opening his hands out. 'I want us to be together, really together ... when can we be together?'

The girl hesitated.

'Are you sure?'

He had no idea, or no time, for all the unspoken apprehension; he was conscious only of an overwhelming desire, the nature of which he did not yet fully understand.

'Of course, of course.' He became impatient. 'When? In London?'

London was agreed on. Two days later Ashley departed home and there settled down to brood upon his new obsession. Obsession was perhaps just the right word, for strangely he found the image of the girl Arlene more vivid in her absence, if that were possible, than in her presence. Often he would be going about his dull tasks and would suddenly find himself falling into a trance-like state, contemplating the startling memorised vision. Did she really look like that? Was she really illuminated as if by some subterranean glow? Or was she some ebony-faced ghost?

When finally they met Ashley found, a little to his alarm, the vision far more disturbing again than the dreams. As he watched her walking down the platform towards him it was like watching a bright ray shining through gloom: but more than that, and this disturbed him though he could do nothing about it, he felt towards her, there in the middle of this busy humdrum railway station and the teeming people around, a savage, almost primitive surge of desire that seemed quite unrelated to anything else. Without stopping to analyse too much he realised vaguely that it had something to do with her coffee-coloured skin, her alien beauty, her secretive quality of being part of some ancient primitive race. When, moving to meet her, he held out his hand and clasped hers, he felt the knowledge of all this coursing through the flesh, like life's blood.

They walked about London for most of the day enveloped in a curious cocoon of unspoken feelings. On the surface, Ashley supposed, theirs was a romantic state. The girl, he realised, was genuinely drawn to him, but underneath he was uncertain, even afraid, of the latent feelings he now experienced. For whatever reasons he found their coming together an irresistible movement towards the inevitable: and at some stage he said almost roughly:

'I want you ... I keep thinking about you all the time ... please ...'

They booked in at a quiet Bloomsbury Hotel, and were shown up to a small but cosy room high up, with a view over London roof-tops. Ashley, who had expected to feel nervous, found all fears brushed aside by a more primitive urge. He went over to the girl, standing by the window, and took her in his arms. She looked at him curiously – afterwards he wondered if in some way she had expected him to say something – and then, so far as he was concerned, she became some strange, exotic object of which he took possession. It was exciting and erotic: he was reminded from that very first time of being an explorer in a jungle, uncovering the foliage and palm-leaves, penetrating to the heart of some weird, tribal centre ... It seemed almost as if, despite herself, the girl reverted to her own shadowy background, becoming something of the animal she had tried so hard to escape from. At least, that was how Ashley rationalised the fierce blaze of their lustful love-making.

Afterwards, lying naked on top of the bed, she rubbed her marvellous coffee limbs against him and murmured:

'Do you love me?'

'Yes,' he said, almost absent-mindedly. 'Of course I do.'

The strange pattern of their relationship began to unfold from that afternoon. There were other, similar occasions, spread over weeks and months. They became like a drug for one another, but for different reasons. The girl seemed to be drawn to Ashley on a different plane altogether. She spoke frequently of love, of partnership, of mutual plans together – if Ashley had not been so blindly obsessed he would have recognised that she even thought about marriage. As it was, in reply to all these things, Ashley had the ready retort: 'Yes. Of course I love you. Very much.'

And all the time, on his own plane, matters were taking a more tortuous course. It often seemed as if every time he touched her, even every time he saw her walking towards him, she reminded him that perhaps he was disorientated – that really he did not exist here in some suburban street, but somewhere quite different, some wild, uncultivated sort of place, where the law was of the jungle, not of man. These were not thoughts which would normally have occurred to a man like Ashley, who had previously led a fairly blameless, indeed colourless life – a life in which his contacts with girls had been decorous beyond belief. No, he decided, it was really the girl's own fault. There was some quality about her which reached through and stirred up some troubled corner of his own being ... so that when he met her he was eternally restless, pacing up and down like an animal, clutching and unclutching his hands as if in some private paroxysm of pain – until at last the thing became unbearable and, turning, he would seize hold of the girl and begin shaking her, backwards and forwards; then clasping her to him, forcing her body into the outline of his own, as if determined to mould her being into his inner self.

After a while the girl gave up her job in Liverpool and came to live with Ashley in London. They found a small basement flat in the Notting Hill district and for a long time this became not merely their home, but their secret world. What went on outside, their jobs, their journeys, was of no importance: what happened once they closed the front door behind them was all that mattered.

Although now living together, they remained subtly apart – on Ashley's part by choice, on the girl's part unhappily so. Not altogether aware of her own sensualities she continued to be drawn to Ashley for some vague qualities of romance, of kindness, of friendship, which were mostly of her own imagining. Coming, as haltingly she sometimes explained to Ashley, from an emigrant West African family who had endured slum conditions for many years in Liverpool, she had fought hard to emerge into what she considered the environment of a civilised people. Now really all she wanted, all she asked for, was this very thing – a contented relationship with a man she loved.

Ashley never asked her if she loved him, he took it for granted – more than that, it was of little interest to him. What really interested him lay beyond such a genteel veneer ... It emerged sometimes deep in the dark night when, perhaps having stayed up late sitting by the fire, he turned and suddenly saw the brown ebony shape beside him, curled up in some insinuating and provocative pose. It was easy in the dim light to imagine some other kind of life, the cawing of birds in the trees, the slithering sound of animals slinking through the bushes, the menace of the unknown. Each time, now, that he reached out to encompass the warmth of her flesh, it was with a grip harder and more insistent, even cruel or brutal. But the girl, because she wanted to please him, forced herself to resent nothing, to accept everything; responding, always responding, to each new whim, even the indignities. And curiously, because she played the part, so, subtly, she became the part, in a way that could hardly be explained; but once accepted, could hardly be forgotten again, either.

In this way they ensnared one another into an increasingly bewildering mesh of mysterious circumstances, the one clear result of which was that they were lost, drowning in deep seas. Once or twice, perhaps, like a drowning person, one or other might try and protest, raising a weak signal of despair. 'A child ... I would like us to have a child,' the girl whispered one night into Ashley's sleepy ears ... and the thought whirled round his head worryingly until he assimilated the full significance, and then almost shouted: 'No – no, not a child.'

But it was not that, but something different that brought the affair to its almost ritualistic climax. The instigation came from Ashley: the culmination from the girl. In Ashley's case it came at the end of a long, troublesome period, during which he went about in the daytime with his mind in turmoil, contemplating the possible evolution of their strange relationship. He had taken to haunting second-hand bookshops and brooding through books about life in Africa among the native tribes. Sometimes, particularly with the illustrated books, he would spend an hour just reading and staring at the glimpses of an alien world, that was now strangely familiar. And now and then, when he came across a glossy photograph of some native girl dancing with wild abandonment in the centre of some village square he would find himself, alarmingly, seeing some other image over that figure – the image of an even more exotic, and more familiar figure.

One night, after reading one of these books, he waited until they had gone into their small enclosed bedroom and then said thickly:

'Dance for me.'

'Dance?'

'Yes ... undress and dance.'

It was a measure of their involvement that she did not make any protest or seek any explanation. After a while she took off her clothes – a series of movements he always watched with fierce pleasure, for with each removal it was as if she was doing more than taking off her clothes, was in fact stripping herself each time of one more layer of convention.

Then, when she stood by the fire, naked, she began slowly to move round and round in what at first could hardly be recognised as a dance and which yet subtly – with an ease which surprised even the girl herself – began to change into a recognisable ritualistic sort of movement.

Ashley sat in the shadows, watching, silent; and the girl danced on and on and on ... At first she had been possessed by conflicts of ideas and images and ethics; but curiously, the longer she danced, the more she whirled herself out of one world into another – the more she changed, even in appearance, from someone who might be just another girl, to a special kind of woman, an animal-like virtuoso, a human tornado of rippling torso, ebony-hued arms whirling, sinewy legs twirling, the whole given up to some private ecstasy of dance, dance, dance!

At first it seemed as if the girl might dance all night, forever and ever. In the end Ashley said curtly: 'Stop – stop now!' – and in the middle of some wild movement the girl stopped, just like that. She looked about her with drowsy, heavy-lidded eyes; lost, utterly lost.

'Come here,' said Ashley, in the same curt tone: and in the same drowsy manner the girl came over and offered up her sweating body to his fierce embraces.

After that it seemed the progression went on at a hurried pace. Night after night Ashley demanded that the girl danced, and night after night the girl did as she was told – in some way seeming to enjoy, even if painfully and perversely, the new trend of their relationship.

At last, caught up as if by some tropical fever, Ashley goaded himself, as well as the girl, to a point beyond endurance. One afternoon browsing among some second-hand stalls in Portobello Road, he came upon a sight that should have seemed strange, but suddenly seemed almost familiar – a long brown leather whip, with great curling thongs. Ashley could not take his eyes off the whip, staring at it bemusedly until the stall keeper came over.

'Nice little thing, ain't it?'

'Yes, it is.' Ashley hesitated. 'Is it – is it African?'

'That's right, mister. Genuine African – from the land of the tom-toms.'

He bought the whip for some quite small sum and took it home. At first he said nothing about it, but nursed the knowledge to him like some viper in the bosom. Only when they were in the bedroom that night did he take it out, quietly and purposefully, and lay it across the smooth white cover of the bed.

He sensed, without seeing, the girl's reaction. He heard her stop in her movements, and the hiss of air that escaped through her teeth. He turned quickly to look at her and saw her lips drawn back, almost as if in some emotion more fearful than fear itself. For the first time he saw a sight which perhaps subconsciously he had been wanting to see all the long time he had known the girl – from the first moment he had set eyes upon her across that room full of dull civilised people. She looked – yes, he thought with a strange, secretive satisfaction – she looked like an animal, a hunted and cornered animal.

Without saying anything Ashley picked up the whip, liking the feel of the rough leather against his fingers. He began stroking the thongs, aware all the time that the girl was watching, mesmerised. Then, slowly, he began to move towards her.

'You're a bad girl, aren't you?' he said in a guttural voice. 'A bad girl ...' Suddenly out of some distant past the word came to his lips. 'A bad kaffir girl ...'

Then he lifted the whip and cracked it viciously across the girl's bare back, leaving a long red wheal.

The girl gave a cry of pain, but made no movement. Ashley raised the whip again and struck, and again the girl cried out. He struck again and again, each time with increasing force ... and each time the girl's cry was louder and fiercer ... yet at some point, subtly, intermingling pain with something like ecstasy.

At last, suddenly disgusted with himself and the whole situation, Ashley flung the whip away and stood breathing heavily. Moaning to herself the girl slid to the floor and then crawled towards him. While he watched as if in a trance the girl nestled against his feet abjectly ... and then, like any slave might have done to her hated master in the past, she looked up with heavy, lack-lustre eyes. Ashley was never to forget the utter blankness of that look, the sudden lack of any sort of communication.

Wearily he dragged himself to bed, leaving the girl where she was, crouched on the floor like a dumb animal. For a long time he remained vaguely aware of her heavy, disturbed breathing ... then at last he slipped off into an uneasy, dream-haunted sleep.

When he woke up in the morning, there was brilliant sunshine flooding into the room – illuminating its strange emptiness. He looked around, startled. There was no sign either of the girl or her few belongings. Alarmed, Ashley jumped out of bed and began searching around the room. On a table by the door he found the brief note: 'I am going back to Africa.' It said little – and yet, there, it said everything.

Through the long interminable day Ashley lay on the bed staring up at the ceiling, trying to summon back the last visions. Dimly he began to understand that he had done something terrible, not merely to himself, but to the girl – and knew he would go on comprehending this, with increasing clarity, for the rest of his life. Towards evening, he dressed and went out into the streets, and began walking about aimlessly. It was almost as if in a way he was searching for the girl, though he knew only too well that she had gone forever. With her, too, perhaps had gone all manner of marvellous and magical things ... the memory of which lay waiting to taunt him for the rest of his life.

X

The Weekend Escape

I often remember how my wife and I first saw the cottage. Everything was still and quiet and peaceful, just the gentle murmur of a breeze in the early green leaves of a secluded West Country wood on a spring day – and there, tucked discreetly among the trees so that only the sharp-eyed like us could see it, stood a neat red-brick cottage.

'Look!' hissed Sylvie, her lips parted excitedly. 'Isn't it heavenly?'

What's more, it was not only heavenly but apparently unoccupied. The front door was locked, but we were able to peep through the windows and make out the shadowy outline of a sitting room and a kitchen and small dining room, and upstairs it looked as if there were three small bedrooms. There were curtains on the windows and the rooms appeared to be furnished, but everything had the appearance of not having been lived in for a long time.

'Darling,' said Sylvie in a tone of wonder. 'Do you think there's a chance?'

We went there and then to the nearest village and made our eager inquiries. The truth was we had been dreaming our private dream of a cottage in the country ever since we got married. If nothing else it helped to give zest to our Sundays, most of which were spent on questful walks about the countryside, or as much of it as was still undisturbed by the erosion of twentieth-century progress.

What we were looking for was some snug little place which we could rent as a week-end escape from workaday life in the Big City. As Sylvie had kept on a very good secretarial job and I earned a reasonable wage in a publisher's office we always felt our dream was a practical possibility, but after innumerable disappointments we were beginning to give up hope.

Suddenly, miraculously, the dream was a reality. After being shunted from one village dignitary to another we finally tracked down the owner of the cottage, a local farmer, who startled us by agreeing on the spot to let the cottage on a yearly lease.

For the rest of the next week we went about in a daze, sometimes pinching ourselves to make sure we weren't dreaming. A cottage in the country! Far from the madding crowd … a cottage of our very own!

'I can't believe it,' said Sylvie one evening as we sat excitedly planning what we would need to take down with us. 'I just can't believe it.'

But it was true enough, we realised the following Saturday morning as we stood proudly at the doorway of our new week-end home. This was our very own cottage in the country.

We would have expressed our happiness with more abandon if we had been alone, but as it happened we weren't. We had with us Sylvie's father, Mr Hinckley, who the moment he heard our news had insisted on driving us down in his large and rather ostentatious modern saloon car.

'There's really no need,' I had said on the phone. 'We can easily go in our old bus, you know.' I gave a deprecating laugh. 'I'm sure it will get us there.'

'Don't be silly, lad,' said Mr Hinckley, who had no sense of humour. 'Can't trust an old wreck like that – travel in comfort, that's what I say. Besides …' At the other end of the phone I could imagine Mr Hinckley's bushy eyebrows going rapidly up and down. 'I've had dealings with the building trade; you never know, I might be able to make some suggestions.'

So now Mr Hinckley was with us, bluff and bowler-hatted, eyebrows working overtime, sniffing around. So, as it happened, was Mrs Hinckley.

'You won't mind if I bring Mother, will you? Besides, you never know – Mother's had quite a lot of experience of decking out new homes, haven't you, old dear?'

My mother-in-law was, indeed, full of suggestions. She led an authoritative way round the house.

'If I were you I'd repaper that room, and of course that wardrobe will never do – and then look at all the windows – oh you'll need lace curtains for those.'

'But what for?'

'Why, goodness me, think of all the people who might peep in!'

When Mrs Hinckley had finished it was Mr Hinckley's turn. He didn't like the condition of the brickwork in one wall, and had I noticed that one of the doors wasn't properly aligned, and then what about those minute spots on the cross-beam – probably woodworm. Hadn't we better get the place surveyed? You could never be too careful.

After sharing the sandwiches and bottle of wine which, romantically we had brought to toast our secret hide-out Mr and Mrs Hinckley took themselves off for a stroll around the locality, and Sylvie and I were at last left gloriously free to get on with various tasks about the house. We had brought quite a selection of items with us – some pictures, our favourite pottery coffee set, a contemporary bedcover, some other odds and ends – soon the rooms began to take on a more familiar flavour.

We were so busy that we hardly noticed the time flying by – and after all, I thought, what did time matter for the present? That was the whole idea of a week-end retreat, a place where we could forget about time and all our other problems.

Pausing in my domestic chores I tiptoed over to where Sylvie was fitting some new curtains, and crept my arms around her lovingly.

'Happy, darling? Like your little nest in the country?'

Sylvie stirred uneasily.

'Mmmmmh, yes its lovely ... Darling, what do you think can have happened to Daddy and Mummy? They seem to have been gone a long time.'

'Oh, bother your father and mother –' I began.

Sylvie pouted.

'Don't be mean. They've really enjoyed coming out.'

'Oh, I'm quite sure they have. But I –'

I choked back the words as the front door creaked open and in came Mr and Mrs Hinckley. Their cheeks were bright and rosy and they had quite obviously enjoyed their walk.

'Well, well,' said Mr Hinckley cheerfully. 'Some pretty walks around here, I should imagine. I shall look forward to exploring the district pretty thoroughly.'

He advanced into the sitting room and looked around expectantly.

'How about collecting some wood and getting a little fire going, eh? Gets a bit chilly in the evenings in the country, you know. Nothing like a cosy log fire for getting all snug and cosy.'

So snug and cosy did my father- and mother-in-law get in fact that as the evening wore on they viewed with increasing and obvious dismay the prospect of making the drive back to London.

'Why bother?' said Sylvie with a cheeriness I could not share. 'There's a spare-room – you can sleep there.'

Which is exactly what they did not merely that night but Sunday night as well. After all – 'Might as well stay over and run you two in nice and early Monday morning, eh?' said Mr Hinckley comfortably.

At least the following week-end when, somewhat righteously, I had invited my widowed mother down to see our new possession there was no problem about whether she would stay the night – having made a lengthy journey down to the West Country she could hardly do otherwise.

'And very welcome she is, too,' said Sylvie bravely.

All the same I couldn't help noticing that over the week-end my mother, who is used to running her own house on rather rigid lines, seemed to be always in Sylvie's way. In the end I felt bound, tactfully, to urge caution. I drew my mother aside.

'Look, dear, try not to interfere in the kitchen. You know –

too many cooks, and so on.'

My mother sniffed.

'Oh, well, if I'm not wanted ...'

'Don't be silly, it's not like that.'

But there was no doubt my mother took umbrage, and after a while she went out huffily – 'to be out of your way' – and Sylvie and I were thus left alone to develop the row that had been boiling up gradually.

'I don't know why you have to invite your mother up quite so soon – you might have given us a chance to settle in.'

'Well, I like that! What about you? We had *your* mother and father here right from the word go ... And I suppose they're expecting to come down again next week-end?' I glared. 'Well, they can expect again – you'll just have to put them off.'

Sylvie's underlip quivered slightly.

'Oh, so now I'm finding out what you really think of my parents. I do think you're being beastly.'

I looked at her in exasperation.

'And you're being perverse ... Nobody's being critical about your parents. It's just that – ' I made a helpless gesture. 'Well, just that it would have been nice to have a week-end on our own.' I looked at Sylvie pleadingly. 'Just you and I, darling.'

'Oh, darling, yes of course.' Sylvie was in my arms, and suddenly everything felt fine again. 'You're absolutely right,' she dabbed at her watery eyes and smiled bravely. 'Don't worry, I'll put off Mummy and Daddy and we'll have a lovely quiet week-end.'

True to her word Sylvie managed to stave off Mr and Mrs Hinckley though at the cost of some pretty extensive white lying – and the following week-end we made the journey adventurously in our rattly old car.

It was fun to be booming down the little sleepy country lanes, just the two of us. Sylvie looked a real country girl, the wind blowing in her hair, her eyes bright with excitement. We sang songs and laughed, and I must confess I drove the last mile or two with one arm around my dear wife. We were caught up in a gay mood of happiness, full of a glorious sense of freedom ... until, pulling up at the top of the path leading through the woods to our cottage, we found a car already parked there.

'Funny,' said Sylvie, 'I wonder whose it is? Must be someone out for a picnic.'

In a way it was. Only the someone turned out to be Sylvie's brother, Harry, and his wife and their two small children and their pet dachshund dog. Quite a crowd in fact. We had some difficulty in getting them all round the table for a hasty impromptu lunch – and our own food didn't go very far, either.

Mind you, Harry was very flattering about our astuteness in finding such a lovely little cottage. Very flattering indeed.

'I don't mind telling you I'm surprised. I never thought you two would have the gumption. Matter of fact, Ethel and I have had the same idea for years, haven't we, Ethel? Been keeping our eyes open for a little place just like this, yes indeed ...'

As he spoke Harry kept pausing and going outside and standing looking at the cottage from different angles. Something about his manner worried me.

'What's he up to?' I hissed to Sylvie. 'Some mischief, I'll be bound.'

'Tell you what,' said Harry, coming in and putting a large brotherly arm around my nervous shoulders. 'Why don't you and us combine on this place? I mean, it's really a bit big for just the two of you, isn't it? I see there are three bedrooms, so we wouldn't be crowded – you two can have one, Ethel and I another, and the third one for the kids. Be quite a sensible sort of arrangement really. Your Sylvie and my Ethel could take turns in cooking, and then ...' He gave me a nudge and a knowing wink. 'Who knows, you and I might be able to nip down to the local for a quick one, eh? By the way, how far is the nearest pub?'

'Oh, miles and miles,' I said quickly. 'Much too far – you'd never have time to get there, I assure you.'

It was difficult dampening down the enthusiasm of Harry and Ethel, but somehow we managed it. Of course, it took time and they stayed for the whole week-end – after all we felt it was the least we could do, and really it would be a small price to pay for future freedom. Still there was no denying it was rather a strained week-end, and we hardly parted on the best of terms.

'Well, anyway,' I said to Sylvie as we drove back to the comparative peace of our routine working week in London, 'We've more or less run the gamut of relatives ... I don't suppose there'll be any more visitations.'

But I was wrong there. Few bush telegraph systems are more efficient than the family one; during the next few week-ends we received 'casual' visits from one uncle, one great-aunt, and three cousins, all of whom were charmed and enraptured by our cottage in the country – so much so that they could not bear to tear themselves away and slept the night in that large spare room which I had half fancied turning into an amateur work-room.

And then there were our friends. We never knew we had so many. Naturally we had been inclined to boast a little about our prowess in discovering such a gem of a place. Now everyone clamoured to come down and see for themselves – usually begging a lift in our car.

It went on and on – and on and on – and on and on – until finally, one lovely summer morning as, in somewhat lacklustre fashion, we were making preparations for the journey down for a week-end which looked like being shared with one or other or perhaps both lots of our parents, I suddenly paused in the act of packing a suitcase.

'Do you realise,' I said irritably. 'We haven't spent one week-end on our own in that confounded cottage?'

Sylvie nodded unhappily.

'What's more, it doesn't look as if we ever will,' I continued.

Sylvie nodded again. The pair of us stood looking distastefully at the suitcase, and also at the large box packed full of extra food that would be needed to cope with our guests.

Sylvie heaved a great sigh. She came over and leaned her pretty head sadly on my shoulder.

'Do you remember how we used to go somewhere different every week-end? Wasn't it fun?'

'Yes,' I mused. 'Just the two of us ...'

I suppose the penny dropped simultaneously. I'm not sure we didn't give whoops of delight. At all events in no time at all we had pushed away the box, grabbed our own suitcase, and were sitting in our dear old car – heading in quite a different direction to the usual one. A few hours later we were climbing over wild downland, miles and miles from anywhere, feeling free, gloriously wonderfully free – while down at our country cottage, we had a shrewd suspicion, several branches of the family were probably bickering over who should do the cooking and who was going to sleep where.

The next week I put an advertisement in the papers offering to sub-let the cottage. It was amazing how many people wrote in. I couldn't help wondering, as I signed the agreement with one of them, if he had many relatives and friends.

XI

The Dark Room

The room was dark. Dark as the night, dark as the deepest pit. The man opened his eyes and there was darkness, closed his eyes and there was darkness, opened his eyes again and they were swimming helplessly in a vast sea of darkness.

He lay there, straight and silent, acutely aware of a strange, inevitable lack of movement. He tried to think where he was, how he had come to be there, but somehow he could not focus his mind. Each time he attempted to concentrate the vague thought slipped away and was drowned in the darkness.

He had never been in such a dark room in all his life. He was used to brightness, to sunshine in the daytime and bright lights in the evening. He liked rooms with large windows that let in plenty of light, he liked to see the bright colour of life around him. Even when the war-time blackout came he had gone to a great deal of trouble to have thickened curtains installed so that, behind the gloomy exterior, he could live in a world of light and brightness.

Even with the blackout? He grasped the small, single thought in gratitude. He must be in a room in which all the blackout curtains were still drawn. It was a perfectly natural explanation, he thought, feeling the darkness swirling around him restlessly. He opened his eyes again, only more deliberately, keeping them open and striving to pierce the shadows. He could not be sure whether he saw only shadows, or whether he could make out the vague shapes that belonged to a room. One moment he thought he saw the outline of a door, of a window – the next moment he saw huge, shapeless shadows.

He would have to explore, of course – yes, he would have to explore. The curious thing was that, in the meantime, he felt strangely content to lie where he was, still and silent and without effort. It was a luxury, after so much endless movement, to be able to relax, to feel his whole body sinking into soft sleep. It gave him a new and indescribable pleasure to be drowning in the darkness without attempting to escape the slow rolling waves. He wondered why he had never thought of doing it before, he might have saved himself a lot of needless worry and wasted energy. But of course, someone would have disturbed him; Hilda, or one of the children. It was a miracle they had not disturbed him already.

For the second time he grasped a thought, grateful for its falling out of the darkness. His wife and family; they were something real, as integral a part of his life as his own being. They belonged, they must have some relation to him even in this dark unknown room. He thought of Hilda; her round red-cheeked face, her plump warm body, her fierce self-assertiveness that often antagonised him, yet sometimes gave him a possessive thrill. He thought of the endless familiarity of her – her squat nose, her shiny sweatiness, her short noisy footsteps, the tones of her voice – familiar, monotonous things yet, he remembered vaguely, a part of a life, of their life. He was glad he had married her, glad to be able to feel her presence in his life ... Glad of the children, for all their pasty faces and eternal questions ... She, and they, were links in the chain. It was comforting to have a chain to grasp in a life of uncertainty.

The soft cloak of the darkness broke, speared by a pang of worry. A faint, itching worry that was just enough to irritate him, to scratch at his soothed body, to stir him in the sleepy darkness. He became aware, suddenly, of a new urge, a new spark of strength. He decided that if he took things easily and carefully he would be able in a moment to sit up, to swing his legs to the ground and make his way over to the door of the room. It would require a tremendous effort, but would win a great reward. He thought beyond the confinements of the room, to Hilda, to the light. He found it difficult to retain the thought consistently, sometimes it whirled out of his mind and became mixed up with the darkness – or perhaps it was the darkness that swirled in and out of his mind? – but he kept his mind fixed intensively on the thought, fixed on the faraway image of his wife, with her round red smiling cheeks.

When he began to move he became confused. He had a curious feeling – the darkness, of course – that his limbs were moving, yet that he himself was not moving. Yet he was conscious, as if of the rapier thrust of fire, of the touch of his hands on the darkness. It seemed that while he lay there in drowsy immobility, another part of him, his short, uneven stubby fingers, travelled out into a dark unknown world, prodding its elastic mystery. Prodding ... prodding ... prodding ... prodding ... but reaching to what? His fingers, clawlike, pressed only into the depthless, empty darkness. It must be a very large room, he thought (and yet I'm sure it's a very small room, he thought). It must be a very wide room and a very long room and a very high room, he thought (and yet I'm sure it's a very small room, he thought). The darkness clung and tugged at his fingers ... Yet, somehow, so dark was the darkness, so large and empty and unresponsive was the room, it was quite impossible for him to know whether he was in fact moving his arms, or whether it was the darkness, and not him, that moved.

The blind must feel like this, he thought; awakening among strange surroundings, bereft of familiar scents and sounds, groping into the unknown, wanting desperately to touch a cornerstone of reality. He was not blind; oddly enough he felt quite sure that he was not blind; but he began to think about blindness because now it seemed real and was something to cling to, was a guidance, a precedent. He was the blind, groping in the harsh, unfriendly outer world. If he groped long enough and far enough he would find something, feel something. Even the blind found their way through the darkness.

He began to wish fervently that there was someone to lead him now out of the darkness. Someone to catch his groping hands, to hold them and pull him gently towards the door and out into the light. He felt, instinctively, that if someone would clutch his hands movement would be granted him, movement to step softly and surely through the darkness.

He began to wish for his wife, for the safety of her presence. The desire seeped out of his body and hurled itself wildly across the barriers of space between them. Hilda, he begged, his crooked fantasy fingers curving her warm shape out of the bloodless dark. Hilda, he cried, his fists beating against bare, hollow, imaginary walls. Hilda, he screamed, aghast when the scream choked and faded and was swallowed silently into the endless silence.

Even the blind at last found a way out, he remembered, becalmingly. Even a room must have walls, must have a roof and a floor, must have windows and a door, he thought, with recaptured cunning. Must have walls, he thought and swung his steel-springed arms backwards and forwards, swinging to and fro and to and fro, like great pendulums. Must have roof and floor, he thought suddenly reaching his arms high up into the sky, then pounding them down like hammers into the earth. Must have windows, he thought, clawing with long dagger fingernails for the strangling curtain and the blue glass panes. Must have door, he thought, pulsing his muscles and smashing great ramming fists into the iron-bolted darkness ...

The great emptiness broke and fell about him in a hundred pieces, only to form its new shapelessness beyond his reach. And now he felt fear; fear that was hidden and buried and slept over, now pricking the balloon of his calmness. Prick, prick, prick ... like the slow, cold, cold drip of water.

Now there was a mental darkness closing around him, like the physical darkness that blinded his outward eyes. Desperately he fought it, urgently seeking the hidden memory. Closing his eyes he summoned up, clear and alight, the hundredfold visions. The father with the wise grey eyes, the mother with the rocking arms, the girl in the orange dress, the long green of a climbing field, the stone grey side of a house; the train rattling over points, the wind across the city square, the river under the bridge; the clatter of typewriters and the singing of the sea; the petulant rhythm of children's voices in sleepy nurseries ... Slowly and ponderously, like the heavy wheel of a water mill, the thoughts and visions began to move, revolving into a huge juggled confusion. Places, faces, movements, voices, songs, whispers, tear-drops, laughters, sudden sharp photographs stabbed bright and alive in the frame of eternity. All tumbling and falling, falling and tumbling, whirling into the great circles of a rainbow; faster and faster and faster.

(To be alone in a dark room, to be swamped in the darkness and drowned in the emptiness, to be groping into an eternity ...? It was not possible, it was beyond possibility. Somewhere, somehow there was a path-way – somewhere, somehow, somewhere, somehow drummed his heart. Somewhere, somehow there was a door – somewhere, somehow, somewhere, somehow sang his memory. Somewhere, somehow there was a light – somewhere, somehow, somewhere, somehow whispered his will.)

Faster and faster and faster; tumbling memories, glories of once upon a time, dreams of times to be, sleeping hopes and shouted regrets; whirling into singleness and oneness and completeness.

And then it came to him, came to the blind, came to the lost, came to the seeking one – a great shining star (the mixture of it all, the rainbow and the raindrops, the red cheeks and the orange dress, the wise eyes and the lulling arms, and the last daddy-cry). A great shining star, aflame in the endless darkness, riding high, and higher and higher. He saw it framed in some far doorway, so that he knew forever that there was a way out of the darkest room, and he called out in joy and surged over the threshold.

Much later, the red-cheeked woman looked for the last time upon her cold, silent man, with his eyes wide open and staring faraway; then she gently closed the door of his coffin, as if she was closing the door of a room that would be forever dark and empty.

XII

The Sacrifice

Mark's Carn stood in a lonely world of its own – a vast landscape of Cornish moors, cleaned almost to the granite bone by the Atlantic winds that whistle over the purple-heather cliffs. From the top, the world below – a huddle of village cottages, a church, some distant farmhouses, cliffs, sea, the smoke of a tramp steamer – all seemed doll-like, unreal. And between this lower world and the Carn stretched all the infinite mystery of the moors, vast in space, shrouded in eternal mists. Only the carn was real, standing high on the moors, chimney stack reaching to the sky, cottage growing out of the wet ground as if it had been there since the first dawn. Here, complete, was a secret place in which anything might happen.

That's what I always thought, from that very first time when Mark and his wife Shelley took me climbing up the steep moorland path. Shelley as a girl's name always used to seem highly affected to me; but not after I met Mark's wife. Somehow it was just the right name for her – small, boyish, puck-faced, with her dark hair cut short. She walked with swift, lithe movements that might almost have been a boy's – yet I was always conscious of her almost feline femininity. Yes, Shelley was her name; it could have been no other.

I didn't know that first day that I was going to fall in love with Shelley. Or did I? And she – did she know? I wonder. The questions hover around like shadows, belonging indeed to that secret world of the Carn. For somehow, once you had climbed over the moors and stood high up, with all that doll-like world spread at your feet, you were inclined to be more emotional, more intense, supersensitive to atmosphere and feeling.

And so, in a way, perhaps there was an immediate contact between Shelley and me – only now, long after, I can't remember it. There's so much in life of that ephemeral nature, which we forget too quickly, and that is so vital in shaping our destiny. I often wonder if Shelley realised just how important our meeting was.

It was a fine, glistening June afternoon when we first went up. I'd met Mark and Shelley in St Ives, an artists' colony on the north coast of Cornwall. It's a gay, colourful place, the houses built around a tiny harbour, with blue and white fishing boats bobbing about like corks. In the little pubs by the wharf, painters and their friends gather in the evenings and argue about Picasso and Matisse and Henry Moore. It's all cheerful and stimulating, and a good way to spend an evening, if you happen to feel in the mood.

But sometimes you don't, and it was on one of these occasions that Mark and Shelley invited me up to the Carn. I was glad to get out of St Ives, sitting cramped in the back of Mark's open car, winding up the long, long hills. I was glad to feel the fresh sea-weedy air on my face, blasting away the cobwebs. I was glad to be heading upward, towards those craggy hills, reaching towards the sky.

Most of all, I suppose, I was glad to be sitting just behind Shelley, so that I could study her profile, the strong lines of her face, the way her nose tilted slightly, the gleam of white teeth between rose-red lips. She was beauty, sheer beauty, the beauty of those very hills and granite cliffs – clear, exquisite, ageless. I did not at that stage reflect about the other side of the coin – that granite is hard, the rocks cruel, the hills remote and uncaring.

We left the car just off the coast road, and walked across two fields and up the steep path that led to the Carn. When we reached the top, there was the cottage – a long, rambling, intimate sort of building that for all its remoteness suggested warmth and comfort. Inside it was all that it promised. The walls had been whitewashed and decorated with modern paintings, and along the shelves stood delicately glazed pieces of local Cornish pottery. Two or three couches, covered in richly coloured hessian, and a thick white rug in the centre gave the main room an air of luxury – into which, I noted at once, Shelley fitted perfectly.

I expect I was shown round the rest of the cottage – the two small bedrooms, the kitchen with its old-fashioned Cornish range, the long, low veranda room which Mark used for storing his archaeological finds – but I don't really remember. What I remember most clearly now is the three of us sitting around the big granite fireplace, drinking first tea and then bottled beer, and talking all the time. And I remember Shelley curled up on the white rug, rather as a cat, suddenly stretching herself in that same feline way, so that under her sweater surged all the hidden beauty of her living body. And I also remember how I wanted her so desperately, so irrationally, that I had to turn my head away and stare blindly into the unlit fire.

That was how it began. I became friendly with Mark and Shelley: with Mark because it was polite, with Shelley because at least it enabled me to be near her, often. I pretended an interest I really did not share in archaeological explorations, and accompanied Mark on several little expeditions among the Penwith Hills. As a trained archaeologist, he was much in demand, and there was a certain interest in accompanying him, for he explained so much that would otherwise have been a mystery. I think that side of the thing attracted Shelley too, for a while. And we had some pleasant times, the three of us, camping out beside some trench-scarred patch of land, out of which piece by piece, we were uncovering the everyday utensils of a bygone age.

Then Shelley stopped coming, and with that, my own interest waned. I knew by now, of course, that I had fallen madly in love with her, but as yet I did not quite know what she felt. I could guess at her awareness, from an occasional exchanged glance, a sudden interrupted reverie. But – I could not be sure.

When Mark went off on his next expedition, which would keep him busy for nearly a week at the other end of Cornwall, I made up my mind to find out.

Waiting until it was nearly dusk, I caught a bus from St Ives to the nearest crossroads, and then walked a mile or so over the fields and up to the Carn. There was a light burning in the dusk, which helped to guide me; though I was so familiar by now with the track that I felt I could find the way blindfold (and indeed there was a curious, faint aroma associated with the Carn, as if, even amid so much fresh air and clean winds, there remained the musty tint of old granite and ancient mortar. And perhaps, who knew, what memories of past occupants? For up at the Carn, one actually felt the belief that anything was possible).

Just as I reached the porch of the cottage, the door swung open. Shelley stood framed in the doorway, the light behind lending a tinge of fire to her ghostly shape.

'Hullo.'

'Hullo ...'

Somehow it was all said, in those two simple words, in the passive way she stood aside, in the positive way I strode in. For a time we stood passing conventional remarks, almost as if others, or at least a third person – Mark – might be present. All the while, I remember, Shelley walked restlessly about the room, and again I was reminded of the rootless, apparently purposeless way in which a cat will pad about – until suddenly it freezes, silently, and pounces.

'Can you imagine what it is like to live here?' said Shelley abruptly, swinging round. She stood in the centre of the room, dark mystery against the blazing-white rug. She had somehow become like the hills, the Carn, remote and complete: a world of her own. It was impossible to associate her with Mark, with anyone; she so obviously belonged to no one.

'At first I didn't mind, the solitude, the loneliness. It was new, and in a way exciting. Then I began to notice things –

about the place, I mean. There was a feeling – I can't think of any other word. A primitive sort of feeling – do you know what I mean? Something to do with age, the past, what's buried in the stone. Mark says ...'

Shelley paused suddenly and looked at me with round, wide eyes. Large, luminous, green cat's eyes.

I never knew what Mark said, nor did I care. I think perhaps she had begun the sentence without intending to finish it, knowing that the spark would light the bonfire.

I took her in my arms. She was all flesh, soft warm flesh that melted toward me. Her face bent toward me, smiling, the eyes bright, the teeth parted. I felt in her a surge of passion against my own desire. As we kissed, I imagined that I encompassed in my embrace all of her, the whole mystery, forgetting that no woman was ever so captured, and least of all this woman.

And yet ... How much do we delude ourselves? Even now, when I remember, it is the light I look for, rather than the dark. When I think of Shelley, it is of the girl I knew in those previous few days – a taut, vital girl, wearing blue jeans and an old fisherman's jersey, with a garland of sea pinks wound into her hair. She was, to me, beauty incarnate. As we wandered about the lonely hills, the sun beating down, the air humming with heat, I marvelled and rejoiced at her presence. To feel her hand in mine, was to feel warmth and passion, ecstasy. Swept up, consumed by such emotions, it was impossible to think of anything else: Mark, for instance.

Does that seem inhuman? Somehow, that world of Shelley's and mine was inhuman. You could almost feel it in the atmosphere all around. Something aloof, something pitiless. The Carn was desolation, a place of lost souls – to exist there you had to snatch, hold hard to happiness.

'Are you happy?'

It was a question I asked ceaselessly, and it was never answered.

'Why analyse? What is happiness?'

And Shelley would look at me with her deep, sea-green eyes. I used to tease her about them.

'They are mermaid's eyes. You have come up from the sea.'

'Perhaps I have.'

Meditative, she had a cool, quiet beauty. It was difficult to believe that fire and passion lay below. Looking at her, I could seldom resist touching her to prove to myself that she still lived and breathed – and the touch was itself like fire.

Then, of course, I saw only one Shelley. I did not know there were others, each one unique, complete, and indestructible. Perhaps that was the trouble: one could not accept the fact, one could not resist trying to destroy all those other, shadowy figures. Until at last ...

During those few days, Shelley and I were lovers. There were no pretences, no half-measures. For a time, the rest of the world did not exist. We made love, we laughed, we wandered, we sat by the fire in the evenings. It was idyllic; I can never forget it. I cannot believe, even now, that it had no meaning for the way she rested her head on my shoulder, or some other unexpected touch of affection, as she passed me in the cottage. But then, that is how all lovers remember, isn't it? A sweet memory.

On the fifth day Shelley sat up in bed, shook herself, then ran her hands through her hair, as if to brush away cobwebs.

'Darling, you'll have to hurry and clear out. Mark's due back this morning.'

Even put baldly like that, the sentence does not convey the full impact as I felt it, that morning. It was spoken so naturally, with such lack of doubt, that it was almost impossible for me to speak in answer. But – what – why? How could any phrase of mine seem anything but humiliating?

I got up without a word, dressed, and went downstairs. When a few minutes later Shelley came down, I was wandering restlessly about, trying to compose myself. It seemed to me she could not possibly comprehend how much she had hurt me.

'Shelley,' I began desperately, 'what are we going to do? I mean ...'

She went and curled up on one of the settees. 'Give me a

cigarette, darling, will you?'

I handed her one. She lit it and puffed up a cloud of smoke. As if mesmerised, I watched the little cloud rising up until, almost imperceptibly, it vanished.

'Darling, don't be a bore.'

'But, Shelley. I mean ...'

I floundered. It was hopeless. At length I spread my hands out in a gesture of despair.

'Don't these past few days mean anything?'

Shelley took a slow puff at her cigarette.

'Of course they do, silly. It's been lovely. But the fact is even lovely things come to an end. And I'm expecting Mark back at eleven o'clock. Don't you think, under the circumstances, it would be tactful for you not to be here?'

I gave way then to humiliation.

'But – when will I see you again?'

She shrugged. Sitting felinely on the couch, Shelley shrugged.

'I don't know, darling. But we'll fix something ...'

I think it was then that I first began to hate her.

The next few days were horrible. Despite myself, Shelley had become an obsession. I could not keep away from her, even though – indeed, immediately – a part of me had recognised the folly and hopelessness of it all.

It was not only a lingering desire to be near her. There was also a morbid fascination. I wanted to be able to be there when Mark was there, and to think secretly – ah, little do you know.

And more than that – well, perhaps, you might say, I had some queer intuitive foreknowledge of what was to come.

And what was that? How can I best describe the process of events? It was like the stitches in some old tapestry, inserted thread by thread, pattern by pattern. Altogether, the events spread over a year, perhaps a little more. I remained friendly with Mark and Shelley, a constant visitor. Every now and then Mark went away. And each time he went away ...

Well, in St Ives there was a wide assortment of attractive men – painters, sculptors, writers, sometimes a fisherman. Perhaps it sounds incredible, but I witnessed all this, because I made it my business to follow to the bitter end my betrayal. During that year, Shelley had several lovers, of whom I was merely the first. She was, in fact, a natural nymphomaniac, completely self-possessed and totally unconcerned with anyone's feelings save her own. Thus equipped, she was able, adroitly, to manage a number of affairs, each one of which, I do not doubt, appeared to her chosen companion as something unique and wonderful.

And Mark? Was he really so unperceptive, so stupid, that he never noticed? Did he ever wonder how his attractive wife spent her time during his absence? Did he, in fact, suspect? About that I did not know. I wondered, I tried to guess, but I could not be sure. My very curiosity prompted a new interest on my part in Mark, and I tended to spend a good deal of time in his company. His attitude, apparently, was as friendly as ever. A big, rather shy man, with a reflective and guarded manner, he was a difficult person to pin down. Indeed, I often felt, exasperated, that if I were to ask him point blank: Do you realise your wife has deceived you not once but many times? – he would have looked at me cautiously and said slowly, 'Well, I'll have to think about that.'

Rereading that paragraph, I am conscious of my failure to give any sort of clear picture of Mark. And yet, in a way, he was the rock around which the pieces revolved. Despite all that happened, Mark was always Mark, pursuing his occupation, living intermittently at the Carn; and Shelley was always his wife. Looking back, I can see there a clue to the whole thing. In a way it was Mark's very solidity, perhaps his stubborn acceptance, that provoked Shelley into fresh outbreaks – and yet, tenuously, held her captive. If Mark had been different; if any one of her lovers had been a stronger, or even weaker character – if Shelley herself had not been Shelley! But then ...

Sometimes I accompanied Mark on short explorations in the Penwith Hills. There was Chysauster Settlement, an old

Celtic site, where you could follow the outlines of ancient encampments. And further along the coast there was a deep pit at Gwithian in which unfamiliar pieces of pottery and other old utensils had been uncovered. Watching the reverent way in which Mark handled these, the real excitement in his usually unemotional face, I gained some clue to his inner character. I learned slowly that a part of him – perhaps all, who knows? – lived in this Celtic past, this world of primitive, yet cunning people who lived by different gods, different values.

One day Mark took me up Trencrom Hill, a great bare plateau, spattered with huge boulders.

'This is where the ancient Druids used to practise their rites. Terrible rites ... yet in a way beautiful.'

I watched Mark curiously. His face had an almost tender expression. I laughed uneasily.

'I can almost imagine you as one of the priests.'

'Can you?'

He looked around slowly. It was a bleak, lonely place, haunted by unimaginable ghosts. It was, in fact, very like the Carn.

'Two thousand years ago this place was alive. The priests came up that path, then they formed around the big stone. Fires were lit, men carried in the sacrifice. There was the smell of myrrh and incense.' He paused. 'And blood.'

I looked around. I felt a shiver of fear.

'What was the sacrifice?'

Mark stared at the flat stone, now covered with moss and weeds. It was not difficult to imagine the scene – the flames, the writhing figure.

'A woman,' he said shortly.

I found it difficult to forget that day, that visit. Every time I visited the Carn after that, I remembered Trencrom. And looking round I thought: this is the same, this belongs to that world. In my mind's eye I saw the priests coming up the hillside in their long berobed procession. Priests! Priests of darkness, rather. And yet, the very hint of evil and devilment held its own fascination.

I began to study the subject. I got one or two books out of the library. One writer described, among other pagan rites, the Black Mass. It was a vivid, excellent description, horrifying, yet fascinating. I was not surprised, reading on, to find that some of the customs had lingered in Cornwall. Cornwall, this brooding land of ancient ghosts, flaked with ghoulish memories, was the home of all that was mysterious and inexplicable.

Up at the Carn, I would talk for hours to Mark. My interest was toward the dramatic, the sensational. I became far more emotional and excited than Mark, who retained something of the scientist's attitude. So I suppose it was my influence, really, that aroused Shelley's interest. I think, too, she was bored, bored with her succession of secret lovers, with her pursuit of pleasure. Secret that is, one assumed, from Mark. Almost everyone else seemed to know. And yet, in a curious way, there was the feeling that the situation, intangible, almost unreal, would continue indefinitely, perhaps for ever.

'These Druids and their performances sound fun,' said Shelley one day, curled up on the sofa, smoking.

'Fun?' said Mark. 'I'd hardly call it that.'

'Perhaps,' I ventured, 'if one uses a little imagination ...'

'Mark hasn't any.' Shelley's green eyes seemed to narrow, as she contemplated some future scene. 'I say ...' Into her voice crept the lilt of excitement, and her lips pouted – at once she was vivid and alive, as she was when she captured men's eyes, hearts, bodies, and souls. 'What about having a party here at the Carn – a sort of pagan party?'

Well, it was her own suggestion. That at least I can vouch for, I wonder though, sometimes, whether words are put into our mouth by other forces? Or even, other minds?

'We could dress up.' Shelley was bright with enthusiasm. 'The St Ives crowd would love it. Think what Rudi would look like as an old priest – and Elly. And Vernon and Max, and Perrys ...'

She elaborated, weaving fantasies that caught at her imagination. Gradually, even Mark took to the idea. A sort of

Ancient Britons' party at the Carn. Yes, it wasn't a bad idea.

It was not a bad idea at all. It had verve, originality, and a sort of morbid attraction. Behind the jovial conception of dressing up, having long beards, wearing costumes, lay a secret curiosity. Celtic rites – black magic – pagan rituals ...? The art students of St Ives, the painters and their mistresses, the fringe of that crowd – everyone caught excitedly at the new bubble. By the time the date of the party was fixed, it seemed that half of St Ives would be coming.

And on the night itself, that weird, unreal night, the lights of cars streaming out along the coast road seemed never ending as they climbed up the hill and parked on the grass verge below the Carn. I counted nearly twenty as I stood down there holding a storm lantern to help the guests across the bracken slopes of the moor. Everyone was dressed up, of course, though not always exactly in the correct period. They made a bizarre group, as they wended in single file across the moor, and up to that remote cottage where Mark and Shelley waited, in a room garlanded with honeysuckle and heather, and lit with candles and flares – while outside, on a plateau just above the cottage, stood the sacrificial stone, a flat white slab which Mark and I between us had rolled down the hillside and polished clean. But of that, for the moment, we said nothing.

Inside, there was hot punch and plenty of other drinks waiting for the visitors. Mark and Shelley made good hosts, passing round continuously and ladling out fresh cupfuls of the hot, invigorating punch. I remember watching them for a moment, standing in the shadow of the door – and for a moment wondering, hesitating. There was something intrinsically honest and good about Mark. How had he been drawn to a woman like Shelley? Was there something in her that he saw, that no one else saw? How could there be? Had I not known her too, as intimately as one can know any human being? Wasn't she, indeed, as she seemed: the eternal, feline, faithless, utterly pitiless cat?

Then I got swept away into a chattering group. There was

Rudi, the sculptor, a lion of a man with grandiose gestures, majestic, wild ideas; his wife Elly, gypsy-like, with long earrings and sharp brown eyes, curiously kind and gentle; Mervyn, a painter, Welsh, a true Celt, with his soft, musical voice; and Tom and Vernon and Angela and Guido and all the other gay, light-hearted visitors. Their punch glasses emptied, were filled, emptied, were filled. Soon the chatter of voices rose up in a crescendo of jovial sound. Before long, someone wound up the old horn gramophone. The floor was cleared, and couples began dancing.

I stood outside. It was dark and still. Somewhere far away an owl hooted. The moon rose uneasily behind shifting clouds. On such a night, many centuries ago, perhaps others had stood there? I hesitated, uncertain, and looked across at the white gleam of the distant stone.

When I returned inside, the party had become wilder. Under the influence of the punch, people were becoming what they were, rather than what they liked others to think of them. Rudi and Elly began doing a wild Apache dance: soon they would be shouting at each other, perhaps fighting. Vernon and Guido, who hardly spoke to each other normally, now chattered happily in a corner as if freed from some terrible bondage. Husbands and wives danced for a time, then inexplicably became mixed up; the amorous patterns became confused.

But somehow that night – perhaps because it was that night – Shelley caught the eye, as vividly as if she were flame in the dark. She wore a tight-fitting garment, made from old fishing nets painted with phosphorescent green – so that in the candlelight, swirling into a dark corner, she seemed to glitter and glow. I had never seen her look so sensual and lovely, so desirable, so mesmerising. As never before, I was drawn to her as a moth to the light.

Despite all my resolutions, I found myself dancing with her, holding her close, the feel of her awakening age-old memories. For a moment, too, I had the illusion that she melted towards me, that she sensed my feelings and shared them, that we could recapture those brief lovers' days.

'Shelley ... Shelley ...' I whispered in her ear. 'You look lovely tonight ...'

She held her head back and smiled; her eyes shone like the sea at night.

But she didn't reply. She just laughed, a silent, solitary laugh, in which I could not share. We whirled round and round, and the room seemed to turn with us, so that I was hardly conscious of the other dancers, or even of the room itself – as if perhaps we were whirling into space itself. I wish we had. Oh, I wish we had!

I was conscious of a curious pause, a momentary silence, and then there was laughter, all around me. Pulling myself together, I found that I was dancing on my own; that Shelley had twisted and whirled away out of my arms into the waiting arms of another dancer. And I was left standing, looking quite foolish, to the amused glances of those watching.

It was like that all evening – as if Shelley had become possessed by some sly, whipping devil, challenging her to flaunt herself as never before. Drunk she was, no doubt, but as much with bravado as from the punch. For the men she danced with were past lovers, each of them linked to her in some subterranean way, as if I had been linked to her – as, I knew, I still was, even though love might be hate. Is not hate love?

And if we felt like that, each of us, what did Mark feel? I looked for him sometimes out of the corners of my eyes. Once I saw him, bent over the punch bowl. With his false beard he looked indeed like some priest of old. He seemed fascinated, as if he were reading some strange fortune in the rust-coloured surface.

I saw him once again, at a later stage, when the dancing had become wild and furious. He was leaning against the door watching, his eyes a little bright, on his face a faint smile. As Shelley flamed by, I saw his eyes rest upon her, and I wondered how he felt; if he felt as I did, deep down within. But in fact, the look on his face hardly changed; if anything it lightened with a curious sort of tenderness, as if – as if – well, I could not somehow put it into words. Pity? Understanding? Sympathy? Love ...?

Momentarily, I was exasperated. I felt more comradeship with Mervyn, who worshipped Shelley blindly, with Vernon, whom I had seen in tears over his rejection – with any of the dozen or so lovers gathered here, all possessed by demons of love and hate, hate and love. At least their emotions were real and vivid, whereas Mark's – well, I suppose I felt a sort of frustration, because still I did now know, and could not tell.

It was in the early hours of the morning that the party moved to its ordained climax. Somehow word had got around about the weird edifice on the hill outside. Gradually we gathered at the doorway, singing lustily, waving our glasses, and then plunged out and up on the hillside.

What a beautiful night it was! Still and clear, with a moon riding high above trailing clouds. In such a light, the hill, the Carn, the whole scene took on a strange, mediaeval atmosphere. This was no longer our world. It was as if the party had been a transitory preparation for stepping from one generation into another. Now, in the silvery light, and wearing the ancient costumes with the cowls raised to add to the mystery, everyone looked as if he belonged, indeed, to those bygone centuries.

In the weird light, momentarily silenced by the mysterious nature of the scene, we all became quiet, so that the shuffling sound of our feet could be heard, eerily, as we padded over toward the raised, white stone. Nobody quite knew what we were going to do; yet, almost by instinct, we were drawn into a sort of ritual. Without anyone speaking a word, we all gathered in a half-circle around the gleaming white stone.

Then one of the hooded men stepped forward. I recognised Mark's voice as he explained briefly the nature of the pagan rites which we were now to perform in mock fun, the meaning of each act, the importance of the sacrifice – the symbolism of blood.

Was he drunk like the rest of them? I often wonder. His voice did not sound blurred; indeed, it echoed beautifully on the night air. He spoke with assurance and confidence, like one who knew exactly what he had to do.

When he had finished speaking, and suddenly produced from the folds of his robes the long, gleaming, sacrificial knife which I had often picked up in his room, there was a gasp among the onlookers – just such a gasp as one could imagine filling the night air in the times of the pagan Celts.

Mark smiled and laid the knife along the edge of the long flat stone. Then he turned, as if waiting; at the cue, we all turned.

And there was Shelley, pale, glowing, advancing across the grass, her figure even more beautiful, even more ghostly in the faint moonlight.

There was a murmur, then a swelling cry of acclamation. Here was the sacrifice. Perhaps at the sight, something stirred in all our blood and bones, for we all began shouting and crying out, and the mass of cowled figures gathered nearer to the stone. It seemed to me that while we were half-pretending to behave in a pagan way – yet, deep down, we really were experiencing those ancient feelings.

I looked up at the sky. As I had imagined, the great clouds had billowed in, as so often they did with the turn of the tide. Now they bore down thunderously upon the waning moon. In a few moments, the brilliant light would be no more; the darkness would have us for its own.

Mark began chanting some incantation. As he did so, smiling softly, catlike, Shelley climbed up on to the platform. She was very drunk. Her body performed movements, her face smiled, while all the time her deep, hidden being was given up to strange ghosts of a dream world. At least this is how it occurred to me, and how I like to remember.

At a sign from Mark, Shelley stepped up and climbed on to the long slab. With delicate grace, she stretched herself out and lay still and glowing, a shimmering figure of beauty.

It was an unforgettable moment. It was entirely primitive, of blood and the dark, brooding mind – the strange, moonlit scene, the darkness enhancing the whiteness of the stone, the knowledge that well-nigh perfect flesh was lying in offering beauty incarnate, yet devil-made – gleaming and glowing, yet radiating Shelley's hidden, perhaps satanic nature – the woman that was harlot, the cat that was cruel, the devil that was rampant in us all.

It was the moment, too, of decision. I looked around at the hooded figures: this one perhaps Rudi, this one Vernon, that one Guido – standing back a little from the stone, Mark. There was something at once strange and yet fitting in that we, her lovers, should be gathered around that white sacrificial stone. I looked across for the last time at Mark, wondering ...

And then with a weird sense of timing the great clouds reached the moon, swept over its gleaming face, and plunged the hillside into deep and fearful darkness. There was a momentary, terrible stillness. Then out of the night came a wild cry, the like of which none of us had ever heard before – dying away even as it sounded on the still air.

At once, all was confusion. Hooded forms moved frantically about; there were cries and counter-cries. Fear spread like fire among us. Somebody struck a match which flickered out at once. Others fumbled their way back to the cottage to bring lights. At last two of them returned, holding aloft a storm lantern.

The scene that met our eyes was the terrible, final one. On the long, white slab Shelley lay, but now there was a curious stillness about her. Protruding from her breast, still quivering, was the long sacrificial knife. And over her perfect whiteness, with the awful inevitability of a deed done, bright-red blood flowed unquenched on to the white stone and dripped down into the dark earth. The sacrifice had been made.

I have tried, inadequately, to capture the atmosphere of that evening, because in a curious way the atmosphere was everything. The Carn, the strange silence of the hills, the moonlight, the loneliness – these things as much as the drink and the pagan imitations, were responsible for the mood. What the mood was I can only hazard. That it did not belong to our normal, sophisticated world, I am sure. We were all of us caught up by the primitive unknown; our very bodies, as Shelley herself revealed in her behaviour, were possessed by some spirits of old. In such an atmosphere, so stripped of convention and falseness, is it not likely that primeval urges, primitive emotions, would have their way?

It seems a long time ago now, though it is but a few years really. You may remember the case – a difficult one, indeed, for the jury to decide. With so many 'interested parties' present, it was difficult, and in fact proved impossible, to say whose hand murdered Shelley. There were no fingerprints on the knife. No one could say for certain that they had seen the deed done. Some suspicion naturally was turned toward Mark, for in such cases the husband is always suspect. Yet his very real grief, his complete breakdown at the time – these things did not suggest guilt. And though he was brought to trial, no one was very surprised when he was acquitted.

I least of all. For it had become evident to me, even before the night of the party, that Mark loved Shelley with an infinite, unalterable love. I shall never forget his look of tenderness that night, in which there was something so pure that it almost compensated for Shelley's behaviour. At that moment, I must confess, Shelley's fate hovered in the balance, if only because of the strength of her husband's love.

But then – I hated her. And sometimes, don't you think, hate is even stronger than love? It can make a man do anything, especially on the spur of the moment – even murder.

XIII

The Wall

The wall was one of a dozen that neatly flanked the long, narrow back gardens of the terrace houses; like the rest it had stood there for fifty years or more, and quite probably would have remained, upright and impenetrable, for another fifty years. But the builders doing up the house next door had instructions to pull it down and build a new one. This, we gathered, was a job for experts, and we awaited their appearance with some interest.

We had almost forgotten the matter when, one morning, I noticed two strange men prowling round the back garden. They made an oddly assorted pair. One was tall and lean, taciturn-looking, with a long pointed nose, the other short and round, almost like a barrel, practically rolling as he walked. As if to emphasise their differences, the fat man wore a battered grey trilby pushed high up on his balding head, while the tall man sported, of all things, a perky black beret.

Yes, indeed they made a disturbing sight, and I had just opened my window to call out to them when something made me pause. The tall man was leaning, very deliberately, against the wall, seeming to push against it with methodical movements; the fat man with a surprisingly agile effort, had hauled himself on top of the wall and was now pacing intently up and down, feeling for gaps with the pointed toes of his shoes. Of course, I thought: the wall men.

From then onwards they were always, for me, the wall men.

The very term in some way conjured up the bizarre atmosphere associated with their appearance. It was not only the faint eccentricity of their dress, it was the secretive way they came and went, keeping apart from the other men, working to some arbitrary schedule of their own. They were curiously independent of external factors. There was nothing else they could possibly be, I felt, except wall men. However, as it transpired, their Christian names – we never knew or needed their surnames – were Henry (that was the tall one) and Len.

Henry *appeared* to be the directing brain of the outfit. He had a way of waving his long arms violently, gabbling words at a rattling rate and generally giving an impression of a dynamo at full speed; while this was going on Len had a way of spitting sideways, tilting his hat still further back, and knocking one-tenth of the wall down with a single blow of a mallet.

That was in the early, purely destructive phase. After all there couldn't be a great deal of argument about how to knock a wall down and I was, frankly, rather surprised that two experts like Henry and Len should require nearly two days to do so. No doubt, I told myself, they were working to some carefully prepared plan.

Towards the end of the second afternoon I sauntered into the garden to exchange pleasantries. The two men were obviously glad of the excuse to pause and smoke a cigarette.

'Well,' I said, 'I see you've got it down.'

Henry looked disdainfully at the untidy heaps of rubble.

'What, *her*? Oh, she's child's play, ain't she, Len? Child's play.'

Len grunted.

'Why,' said Henry, turning upon me the beaky, faraway look of a professional wall estimator. 'She's a mere nothing aside of that wall out at Cricklewood. Do you remember her out at Cricklewood, Len? A hundred and thirty feet dead, she was.'

Len, on the point of giving another grunt, changed it to a few flat syllables.

'A hundred and thirty *and* three.'

Henry gave an indulgent smile for my benefit.

'A hundred and thirty dead, I think, Len.'

Len spat sideways.

'A hundred and thirty *and* three.'

Something in his tone, in the way the remark was received by Henry, whose tall frame seemed suddenly to wind itself round as if in readiness to spring – something in the way they glared (there was no other word for it) at each other – encouraged me to withdraw discreetly.

When I was safely indoors again, I peeped out. They were going at it hammer and tongs. Henry was getting more and more excited, smacking one fist into the palm of the other hand, jumping from one foot to another – at any moment, one felt, he would snatch his beret off and fling it in rage at his companion. Len, by comparison, hardly seemed to move; but somehow one was conscious of suppressed, rugged resistance. 'One-hundred-and-thirty-*and*-three,' his lips muttered, stubbornly.

Was it possible, I wondered, that two men who could give themselves up with such passion to an argument about a missing foot or two in some distant Cricklewood wall – was it possible that these two men could safely be left to put up a new wall?

It seemed my doubts were justified. When it came to digging a foundation bed for the new wall, Henry obviously thought that a foot down was deep enough. Len insisted on digging down further. Henry refused to help. Len stolidly went on digging. Henry began shouting at him, just what I could not be sure. Advice? Comment? Insults? Yes, obviously the latter, for suddenly Len jumped out of the ditch, grabbed his coat, and waddled rapidly off the scene.

It was a sight with which I was to become familiar. It happened regularly several times a day. After one such episode, in which both men had stalked off, I found the foreman of the builders working inside standing anxiously on the garden steps.

'Why don't some of your men get on with the trench?' I asked.

He looked at me aghast.

'What – without *them* knowing? Blimey, there'd be murder, bloomin' murder. Mister, you've no idea what them two are like. Ruddy prima donnas, that's what they are!'

'Well,' I said, 'I hope you don't mind my asking – but are they really good at their job?'

A look of respect filled the foreman's face.

'Oh, yes, sir.' H'outstanding they are, real craftsmen. Why, do you know, there was a wall they did at Cricklewood –'

I beat a hasty retreat. I suppose the man knew what he was talking about. The next morning, Henry and Len were back on the job, seemingly the best of friends. Moreover, somehow they had finished laying the foundations and started laying rows of bricks, from the enormous piles of new bricks the contractors had dumped at the end of the garden.

Ah, I thought to myself, this is where they display their virtuosity. I settled back, prepared to be engrossed, amazed.

Suddenly all was at a standstill. Henry, having finished one line, wished to start the next with a brick turned on its side. Len would not have this. 'No,' he shook his head, 'No – no – no.' His great solid frame seemed to shake as it vehemently registered the negative.

Henry became more and more agitated. I could see him mouthing reasons, perhaps quite valid reasons, for laying a brick on its side. But Len just went on shaking his bullet-like head.

Suddenly Henry bent down and laid the brick. Len pounced like a cat, seized the brick, and with a swift movement of his trowel, broke it into several fragments.

Henry unwound his tall frame, picked up another brick, placed it in line. Quick as a flash, Len snatched it up and with an imperious movement flung it into the middle of our favourite rose bush.

I decided I had better get down quickly, before worse happened. Even so, by the time I reached the garden, half a dozen more bricks had been freely distributed around the borders. All I could see of Henry and Len were two angry backs, disappearing in different directions.

'Extraordinary,' I thought. 'Quite extraordinary.'

'Perhaps,' said my wife casually. 'That's the way they work.'

Quite suddenly, the whole thing fell into perspective. That, I realised, *was* how they worked. And from the new perspective, I began to see things rather differently. What possible explanation could there be for all these dramatic scenes, these passionate outbursts, these emotional crises, except the obvious one? Henry and Len were not as other men; they were artists, with the artist's temperament – indeed, as the foreman had said, they were in their way, *prima donnas.*

And somehow, now I understood this, the whole affair of the wall became removed to a different and loftier plane. For this was not just any old wall – any more I realised than had been the *Cricklewood* wall – it was Henry and Len's wall, a unique event, upon which all their creative talent was focussed. And somehow, now, the progress of the wall assumed a poetical trend. There would be the swift, breathtaking flow when Henry and Len worked together, bricks falling magically into place, the symmetrical lines coming beautifully into existence – then, without warning, some temperamental blockage, a depressing fall from the sublime to the ridiculous. Isn't that always the way with a work of art?

Perhaps you think I'm exaggerating, romancing? Ah, but then you weren't in my garden on that last day when, miraculously, the new wall stood tall and upright, graceful and strong, waiting for the last few bricks.

I watched Henry and Len as they completed their task. They moved slowly and precisely, slapping in the cement, smoothing it down, laying a brick, patting it into place gently – savouring these last touches. Whether by arrangement or not I never knew, but they managed to reach the end of the line together, and at the same moment each deftly inserted his last brick. The wall was finished.

They stood back, viewing it from various angles, touching it gently with the tips of their trowels, like painters applying their last brush-strokes to some masterpiece. I studied their faces. Henry's beaky lines were creased into a broad smile and he kept nodding to himself: Len, in his stolid, down-to-earth manner, looked well satisfied.

There were no arguments, no fuss. They just picked up their coats and their tools, Henry patted his beret in place, Len tipped his hat back; and then with a nod to us, they marched off down the street.

The foreman came out and stood by me, watching them.

'Bloomin' lark, aren't they?' he said.

But I caught the wistful note in his voice.

XIV

Davy and Megan

Davy Morgan was just turned sixty when his wife died of a sudden heart attack. It was a blow to him, of course, but everything happened so quickly – what with arranging things with the doctor, and arranging things with the undertaker, and coping with numerous well-meaning relatives – that Davy hardly had time to think about his loss, or to feel sad or broken-hearted.

At first, indeed, life was so changed that it was almost like being on holiday. Not that that was the way he expressed it, mind, but there was that sort of a feeling lurking deep down, well hidden by the solemn black suit he decided to wear for the time being. It seemed strange not to hear Megan's sharp, rather querulous voice, breaking into his reveries.

'Davy, man, where are those things I asked you to get? Goodness me, why can't you clear up all your mess after you, now? Ach, Davy, what is it you are up to? Why don't you come and sit by the fire, see?'

That was how it always used to be, not a moment's peace he had ... and now all was quiet and soothing like, and he could mope about the house as he liked. Rather pleasant it was, all his relatives and friends – but no, indeed, not so much *his* relatives and friends were they, mostly a lot of old nosy women who had hob-nobbed with Megan – then he was quite happy to settle down to his new life. It meant he was on his own now, for both his daughters were married and living away, and his only son was with the Army overseas, but he felt sure he was quite capable of looking after himself – and Mrs Owen next door had promised to look in now and then and give the house a clean up.

So, during the first few weeks, Davy enjoyed his hermit's life to the full. Somehow, living with Megan had given him a feeling of inferiority. That sharp look of hers and her ready, biting tongue had never been conducive to his peace of mind. Now it gave him a schoolboy sort of pleasure to live life as he wanted, to do a lot of things that would have drawn much disapproval from Megan. At first, mind, he felt a little nervous. When he luxuriously settled in the best armchair and put his feet up on the edge of the highly polished mantelpiece (a thing Megan would have cuffed him over the head for) he could not stop himself jumping up suddenly as he realised the enormity of his offence, in anticipation of the inevitable storm of rebukes. But when nothing happened he smiled expansively and resumed his position, and began puffing contentedly at his pipe. It was the same with his old boots. Megan would never let him into the house without first he took off his boots and put on his carpet slippers. 'Well, fancy – whatever do you think this is, a stable?' she used to ask. But now he could open the door and walk straight in and tramp all over the house in his boots, and no one to stop him. And very nice and free and easy it was, too.

Only after a few weeks had passed did Davy begin to discover snags in his new Utopia. Looking after himself wasn't the trouble – no, he could manage that well enough, an old man like him wasn't fussy. And he had enough money to keep going, even though Megan's old-age money was stopped, what with the small extra amounts his daughters sent. No, it wasn't anything concrete ... It was just that now it was beginning to seem an awfully long time since there was a Megan in his life. Poor old girl, it had been hard for her to go like that, so sudden, just when she seemed set for a good ten years more yet. Of course, she had been an old nagger, and she had bullied him around a lot, mind. But, see, there was cold he was feeling now when he lay in bed at night, it was

cold and lonely all on his own without the plumpness of
Megan to warm him. She had been a nice round woman,
Megan, and fun to lie in bed with and talk to, for all her sharp
tongue. And there was no denying it had been nice, indeed,
the two of them having a sit round the kitchen table and a
good old gossip about the chapel people. Some good laughs
they had had, indeed. Poor old Megan, she would be missing
those laughs.

It was not long before Davy's memory of Megan had
softened considerably, not long before his new found freedom
began to pall, and he was wishing he could have his Megan
back, with all her faults. The problem weighed very heavily
with him, so much so that one day he decided to go along and
talk it over with Mr Edwards, the preacher at the local chapel.

'Missing her very much I am, Mr Edwards,' explained
Davy simply. 'What can I do, now?'

'Well, Davy, I'm very glad to see such true love showing in
you,' replied Mr Edwards, pleased, and speaking in his usual
rather heavily earnest style. 'And perhaps I can help you.
True it is that your Megan has been taken away from us, but
she hasn't just gone out of your life completely – that you may
be sure about, Davy. All our dear departed ones are
somewhere ... waiting somewhere, watching us, loving us,
helping us. And, look, your Megan must be there somewhere,
too. You do believe that, don't you, Davy?'

'Well, yes –' said Davy slowly, a trifle uncertain, but
unwilling to disappoint Mr Edwards, a good man for whom
he had great respect.

'Well, then, if you believe that, you should know what to do.
What do we all do, when in need, when in trouble? ... Well?
... Why, we ask for help. We pray. And that's what you must
do, Davy Morgan. You must pray. Not just once, or twice, but
many, many times. Pray hard enough, man, and you may be
sure your Megan will come to you and comfort you.'

'Well, that is something for sure,' said Davy, brightening up
considerably. 'Indeed, that sounds reasonable, and thank you,
Mr Edwards. Pray to my Megan I will, indeed.'

All the way home he reflected upon the excellence of Mr

Edwards' advice. Foolish he had been not to think of it before. For had not Megan been a regular one at the chapel all her life? Praying would surely be the best way of reaching her, then. And how he would pray! He remembered the many times, kneeling in the chapel beside the tensely concentrating figure of Megan, when he had been inclined to let his attention wander during the long prayers that (it seemed to him) took up most of the chapel service. Often he had looked about him until he caught the eye of Ivor Griffiths, similarly restless, and they exchanged a solemn wink. But there would be none of that now. Oh, no! He was going straight home to kneel down and pray devoutly to his Megan.

And so Davy began praying. He started last thing at night, wearing his old thick yellow nightdress. He knelt beside the big double bed, bending his head over the part which still bore the years old imprint of Megan's heavy figure. 'Oh, Lord,' he prayed, 'Oh, Lord, please tell my Megan I'm lonely and missing her, indeed. Oh, Lord, please tell her it's cold when I am in bed at night, and say how I miss her warmness near to me. And please ask her to send me a word or two, Lord.'

Very slowly and very solemnly Davy prayed, repeating his words time after time, so that he went on praying for a good twenty minutes or so. Then he stopped and waited, a little afraid of what might happen; but in fact, nothing did happen. Still, Mr Edwards had said it would be no use just praying once or twice, and Davy felt he could see the logic of that. So he began praying at other times, too. He took to getting up after a meal, falling down on his knees in front of the old armchair where Megan used to sit, and praying in a loud monotonous voice, sometimes faintly tinged with petulance. 'Oh, Lord, please ask my Megan to speak to me!'

After supper, when he had had a pint of beer to stimulate him, Davy went the whole hog and recited long complicated requests, prefacing them with the most humble and self-effacing apologies. 'Oh, Lord, I am a wicked, wicked old man, and I treated my Megan too badly, indeed, but please tell her I'm that lonely for her.'

One week, two weeks, three weeks, Davy kept up his

praying, but when he asked Mr Edwards for advice the preacher told him to have faith and keep on praying; and since his missing of Megan had become something of an obsession with him there seemed nothing to do but take the advice. So he concentrated more and more on his prayers – indeed, they became the very centre of his existence. Now Davy gave up as much as half an hour or more to each prayer, hunched on his knees so long that he lost all count of time or of where he was, wrapped up with his prayers and his desire to have his Megan back. 'Oh, Megan, bach, come back to your old Davy!' he pleaded, almost fancying he could see her as he spoke.

And then, one miraculous day, his prayers were answered. After an extra long bout of praying Davy fell exhausted on to the bed, but he had only lain there a moment or two when he heard a strange wailing sound. It was unlike any other sound he had heard, and it made his blood turn a little cold. It stopped, and there was an ominous silence.

'Who's that?' called out Davy. He shut his eyes and clasped his hands together. 'Who's that?' he called again.

And this time, straining his ears as he had so often done before, he heard the trembling voice of his Megan. Faint it was, and not quite human like, but it was Megan's voice.

'Hullo! Megan, bach, hullo!' called out Davy wildly, and indeed, it was Megan answering him and whispering:

'Hullo, Davy, bach!'

Ach, it was a miracle, indeed!

'Megan, Megan!' he cried out triumphantly.

And there it was, he had achieved it. Have faith, Mr Edwards had said, and faith he had had, and now he was talking to his Megan. Davy's broad old face wreathed with smiles.

'And how are you, Megan?'

'I'm very well, I am. And how are you, Davy?'

'Oh, I'm well, too.'

'Not looking so well, though, ask you me!' added his dead wife's ghost voice, and Davy started back.

'No, no, Megan, bach – I'm keeping fine. But I miss you, bach, I do miss you ...' And he went on to avow with passion his love and loyalty to her, and how empty life was without her. 'So cold in bed it is, too!' said Davy with feeling.

After that his long praying bouts were not necessary. Davy found that he had now only to mumble something about 'Lord, can I please speak to my Megan?' and lo! there was Megan's voice piercing the surprising emptiness of the room. After a time it seemed to him that the voice became louder, even more like the real voice of Megan. It was true he could not see her, but there was no doubt that he could hear her. Indeed, sometimes she might easily have been just up the stairs, or in another room.

Once in the morning, once at lunchtime, once in the afternoon, and always last thing at night he got in touch with her. And soon the former ritual had become quite a commonplace thing. What was more disturbing to Davy, however, was the fact that so had the conversations become commonplace and familiar. Little chance had he to guide the astral talks, though his praying invoked them. Megan would start off at once with a sharp 'Well, indeed, late you are today, Davy!' or an admonishing 'Sleepy old man you're looking for sure, Davy Morgan!'

'No, no – no, indeed, Megan!' he would protest, but soon she would be off again on some other tag. 'A fine old mess you're making of our home!' she said one day, and he could only mumble something sheepish in reply, as from long habit, instead of shouting the truth – that he was happy like that. And she seemed to know a great deal more about his life than he told her. 'Watching you I was in the Red Lion this morning,' she snapped one day. 'Stupid old waster you are!' Or, 'Look you, Davy Morgan, that money I left in the tea-chest was not for the likes of you to throw away on the dogs, indeed no!'

Davy did not reply to these remarks but tried to remember that after all he did miss his wife. Ach, but if only she would come back to him for a warm in bed, or a gossip and sit in the kitchen – there, that would be nice, now. But the unfortunate part was that this was just what this ghost-like Megan could not do, as she had pointed out to him with some emphasis when he had inquired into her mobility. Nor would she turn the conversation on to more interesting trends and tell him a bit about her life over there. Indeed, there was still no knowing if she was in the hot place or the good one – and bothered if he could decide to which she belonged, sometimes.

But he stuck it, putting on a consistently friendly front, until his dead wife turned on to the subject of Mrs Owen, the widow from next door who came in to do the cleaning. Mrs Owen was a buxom woman, some ten years Davy's junior, and he liked the look of her well enough. But he was no great one for the ladies, especially at his time of life, and he had no real desire to have another woman's permanent company – apart from which he was getting very comfortably settled into bachelor habits, in many ways.

This was not at all the reasoning of Megan, however. 'Now look you, Davy,' she began one morning. 'What about this Mrs Owen, eh?'

'What about her?' said Davy, innocently enough.

'Yes, well you might say what about her, too. Clever cat, that woman is. But you listen to me, fancy Davy. No more of this shall we have, her gallivanting about my house like she owned it. Do you hear?'

'She only does the cleaning,' protested Davy.

'Only the cleaning, is it?' Megan's voice gave a harsh laugh. 'Oh! All those cups of tea, and all those sit-downs in the kitchen chatting with my Davy – part of the cleaning, I suppose?'

'Oh, well –' said Davy, guiltily. The accusation was true enough, though his intentions were perfectly honourable. After all, he had to have someone for a gossip.

'You see, bach, it's like this –'

But Megan either couldn't or didn't want to see. Her flood of abuse, reminiscent of the old days, left Davy in such a tremble that he could only just manage to drag himself down to the Red Lion for a reviving drink. Glad he was to feel the warm pleasant liquid sliding down his throat, he thought, and he ordered another one. Then, sitting there, strengthened by the drinks, he came to a sudden decision. No more praying.

No more could he stand of this. Megan would have to be given up. True, he'd have liked her back for old times' sake – but more for the loving and cuddling than anything. If all he could have was a silly old carping voice that he wouldn't have, thank you. And on the strength of that resolute decision he ordered yet another drink.

That evening, then, Davy Morgan felt in better spirits than for a long time. He made himself some sausage and mash, his favourite meal; and a big steaming cup of cocoa, and afterwards he settled in front of the fire with his feet on the mantelpiece. Then he had a good long smoke and a listen to the wireless. No more praying for him, indeed. A bit of peace and quiet, that's what it would be from now on. And, come to think of it, damned if he didn't make up a bit to Mrs Owen – not a nagger was she.

After he had finished his pipe he stretched himself comfortably, went upstairs and began undressing. Whistling softly, he turned back the sheets and got into bed. At peace with the world was he. His head, deep into the pillow, began nodding.

'So!'

Davy started up.

'What? ...'

'So, indeed, Davy Morgan. So that's how you're going to treat your poor old dead Megan, is it?'

Davy's heart missed a beat.

'M – M – M – Megan? Is that Megan?'

'Oh, Megan it is, for sure. Your lonely old Megan that you haven't so much as prayed to, tonight.'

Davy swallowed hastily. 'Oh, Megan, bach – terribly sorry am I – not well I wasn't feeling, so –'

'Not feeling well, wasn't he? That for a tale! Cunning old man, that's what Davy Morgan is. Thought he would leave his Megan, did he? No doubt a nice long dream about Mrs Owen you hope to have, eh? ... Oh, nice, very nice, indeed.'

Davy said nothing. There was no need to say anything. Megan's voice did all the talking. It went on and on and on, rising and falling, screeching and wailing, until he thought his eardrums would burst. It reminded him of the big rows they had had when he got drunk after the local football final – only it was much worse. She called him this and that, scathing him through and through, and there was nothing to do but endure it. It was not even like a telephone, he thought bitterly, where he could at least have rung off.

'And listen to me, Davy Morgan!' said Megan, a trifle breathlessly, coming to the end of her tirade. 'You needn't think to get rid of me like that, just not praying.' She cackled. 'Well, well, that's a fine laugh, that is, to think of you expecting to do that ...' And she informed him with great relish that whether he prayed or not, henceforth she would visit him daily. Keep a good eye on him, she would, and see that he didn't get up to any tricks with that Mrs Owen – and tell him off well, she would, if he made a mess of her old house.

In the morning Davy rushed round to Mr Edwards. He had not told the preacher anything about his ultimate success with the praying, but now he poured out the whole story. Mr Edwards listened sympathetically, but looked a bit surprised at the end.

'Why, Davy?' he said puzzledly. 'What is it now to worry you? A lucky, lucky fellow you are!'

'But is there no way – supposing I stopped praying – would we still be re-united?' asked Davy urgently, and Mr Edwards looked at him a trifle shocked.

'Indeed, a fine thing to be saying! ... But you wouldn't be wanting to do that, not really.' He nodded reassuringly. 'No, you be well satisfied, Davy, man. Your faith has broken through – you prayed, and now your prayers have been answered. Like that it will be for always, Davy.'

Davy walked out of the chapel-house as if in a daze. And no sooner had he started walking along the wide dusty road than he heard a mocking laugh in his ear. 'Hope you found some comfort with good Mr Edwards, now ...? Ha! Ha! Ha! Funny it is, indeed! Teach you a lesson this will, won't it, Davy bach?'

Davy went on down the road, his heart growing heavier with each step. 'For goodness sake!' he thought wildly. 'This will drive me mad!'

And as he thought thus, he espied a big furniture lorry speeding towards him, a huge thing that looked a bad one to get in the way of. A flash of last-minute hope entered Davy, a sudden wild idea of escape. As the lorry came nearer he halted, steeling himself to run in front of it when it was almost on top of him. Then, abruptly, he relaxed, his arms falling loosely to his sides, his head bowing. He let the lorry trundle past.

Ach, what use would it be, indeed? he thought morosely. She'd only be waiting for him on the other side.

XIII

The Man With A Future

My friend Alan and I didn't take it too seriously at first when our mutual crony, Ricky, took up astrology. After all, everyone should have a hobby, so they say.

We could even pinpoint when it all began. We had been to a fair, not such an exciting or glamorous kind as in the old days, but pretty tawdry as a whole. Still, there was one relic of the past – a fortune-teller's tent. You know the sort of thing, mysterious and secretive looking place with a shadowy interior. When you got inside there was a swarthy old gypsy woman sitting at a table. Alan and I, we had a quick peep inside and then a bit of a giggle and left it at that.

But Ricky, well you could see he was a little more intrigued. Course, we weren't with him when he had his, er, consultation – but he came out looking quite serious-faced.

'What's up, Ricky, lad?' we said, teasing. 'Going to come to a sticky end, are you?'

Well, it wasn't quite that. But Ricky said, first that the old girl had been surprisingly accurate about some things in his past, which of course impressed him no end. And – and, listen here, she said he was going to be involved in an accident.

Of course, we all had a good laugh at this, and went on round the fair. We had one or two jokes, too – when we went on the Dodgems we kept running into Ricky and calling out, 'There, see, the fortune teller's warning's come true!'

Yes, we all thought it quite a joke, and we laughed about it spasmodically while we went round the fair. In fact we didn't stop laughing and joking – until on the way back Ricky's car took a bend too fast and – craaaassh! — we went straight through some railings and over a hedge into a field. The car ended upside down, and we were very lucky indeed to escape with just bruising and a bit of shock.

After that, of course, Ricky began to take the thing seriously. He started subscribing to magazines and taking huge books out of the local library with titles like *The Astrologer's Vade Mecum* and *Your Tomorrow – Foretold Today*. Almost every day, it seemed, he had hold of some new item. He was always writing off in response to those intriguing advertisements you see in the personal columns – you know, 'Let Madame Veronica advise you about *your* future.'

Astrology, palmistry, tea-leaf reading – everything and anything to do with forecasting your future fate. These suddenly became Ricky's all embracing interest – his hobby, I suppose you might say. Only somehow we sensed that it was rather more than that.

That was the trouble, really. At first, of course, we didn't pay all that much attention to the matter. After all, one's friends are always liable to be bowled over by enthusiasms though usually for a girl rather than a forecasting system.

But obviously we under-estimated the situation, for after a while we found Ricky so wrapped up that he hardly ever came out or bothered to contact us.

This went on for a while, and then just as we were beginning to give him up as a lost soul – Ricky made a re-appearance. I use that word quite deliberately, for the truth of the matter was that somehow, in a way we could not quite define, Ricky appeared – well, as if he was a different person. It wasn't so much anything physical, it was just that he had a totally different set of values. He was no longer interested at all in what went on around him, he wouldn't have noticed if war had broken out, I wager. No, all he was interested in now, completely and utterly, was – the future.

I didn't mind, really. In a way I found it quite stimulating. Once Ricky had got the hang of his subject, you see, he began trying to work things out among his friends. And this – well it kind of made you feel important, even if you didn't agree with a word!

It went like this. First he'd badger us all for the exact hour and place of our birth – then he'd go away and pore over figures for hours, at last returning with a minute analysis of our future. Soon, too, he began character reading. It became impossible for Ricky to introduce anyone in a normal way. Oh, no. 'This is my little Pisces friend,' he would say jovially, introducing his latest girlfriend. Or, himself presented to a newcomer, he would stare quite rudely, and exclaim triumphantly; 'You're a Taurus!'

As I say, I found this all good light entertainment: but not so Alan. It was all anathema to him, for he had a strongly scientific training. It didn't help matters that often Ricky was correct in his surmises.

'Nonsense!' Alan would exclaim irritably. 'Pure guesswork. Rubbish!'

Then one day – I shall never forget it – I heard a knock at my door and there stood Ricky. But what a different, changed Ricky. Not the cheery jovial man I had always known, but a haggard grey-faced worn-out wreck.

I was horrified. I made him come in and sit down, and gave him a drink, hoping it would revive his spirits. But apparently not. He just kept shaking his head and muttering, 'No use, no use.'

'But what on earth's the matter?' I asked.

Then it came out. It seemed he had got pretty fascinated with his pet working out of the future, what with the birth-dates of all his friends and so on he'd accumulated quite a pile of documents. But one evening, for a change, he thought he'd amuse himself by working out his own destiny.

'Amuse!' He gave a hollow laugh. That was an ironic way to put it. For when he went into the forecast minutely he emerged with the shattering revelation – that he had only three weeks left to live.

Well of course my first reaction was to laugh, but I soon saw that poor Ricky had taken the 'revelation' very seriously.

What was more, if it had already had such a shattering effect on him, how was he going to be at the end of three weeks, even supposing there was nothing in it at all?

That was just the trouble. Even my friend Alan agreed with me over that, though he was furious with Ricky for taking things so seriously. We both saw that Ricky was quite capable of worrying himself to death inside the three weeks.

Of course, on reflection I began to have a sneaking sympathy with Ricky. After all if you honestly believe that you're going to die by a certain day it's very difficult to avoid a feeling of going about as a condemned man.

That's just what Ricky did. Everything went by the board. He seemed to give up all hope. Alan and I felt more and more concerned, and we tried to keep him company as much as possible, telling ourselves that once the date was past then surely he would stop worrying.

The night before The Day, I remember, we all had a few drinks. That was when Alan at last lost his temper.

'Oh, you blithering idiot, you dolt, you – you – I'm surprised at you, Ricky.'

I suppose those must have been the last words Ricky and Alan ever exchanged.

I went home and fell into a deep sleep. About nine o'clock in the morning I was woken by the ringing of the telephone. When I answered I heard Ricky's voice.

'Hullo,' I said.

And then (I couldn't resist it).

'Well, you're still alive, then?'

'That's what I'm ringing you about,' said Ricky excitedly. Indeed he sounded quite different to the previous day. 'You see, I couldn't really sleep much, so early this morning I thought to myself, well, I don't know, perhaps I'll have one last check up. Maybe I've made a mistake I said to myself. It's just possible.'

'And?'

'Well, that's just it – I had made a mistake. Not in my calculations, though. You remember I used to keep the sheets with the birthdays all in one pile – oh, a dozen or more? Well,

I know this must sound a bit stupid, but the fact is – I read the wrong horoscope. It wasn't mine at all.'

He paused, and then said in a strange, doomlike way.

'It was Alan's.'

'Well, I'm glad to hear that,' I said, my head throbbing still from the previous night. 'Now perhaps you'll stop worrying.'

'But what about Alan?'

I groaned.

'No, Ricky. Please, not just now. Wait till I've had time to get up and have my breakfast. Bye-bye for now.'

'But don't you see? *Supposing?*'

I groaned again, my head aching.

'Ricky, I just can't think about it now. I really must have time to wake up.'

'But –' I remember Ricky's anguished tone.

'No buts,' I said firmly. 'Bye-bye for now.'

I replaced the telephone with a sigh. Why on earth did Ricky want to sound so urgent about things. Him and his blessed astrology. Blow it all, I was going to eat.

I went in the kitchen and made myself some toast and coffee. When it was all made I brought it back into the dining room and sat down and relaxed with one of my favourite occupations – drinking coffee and reading the morning newspaper.

Casually my eyes scanned the usual headlines. Strike threats, film stars divorced, civil war here, invasion there, another disarmament conference, new cold war threat, a plan for the roads ...

And then suddenly my gaze was riveted by a smaller headline. It was a very minor story, the sort often tucked away at the bottom of a page. The heading read simply: MAN FOUND DEAD.

It was thus that I read of the end of my friend ... Alan. Apparently he had been found in the early hours of the morning by a passing motorist lying at the side of the road. This motorist had rung up the police and when they'd come they'd had a good look round but there was absolutely no clue as to what had happened. Maybe Alan had a scare, but he certainly wasn't injured in any way. No, he was just, unfortunately, very dead – from a heart attack, as the inquest later proved.

Which all goes to prove something or other, don't you think? At least that's what my friend Ricky insists.

And how can I contradict him – now?

XVI

Love Thy Neighbour

While the chairman stumbled through his prepared speech, Christian, standing in careful seclusion at the back of the platform, gave a quick, curious glance into the crowded hall. Vivid scarlet robes wound in spirals around the two stone pillars at either end of the platform; long creamy tapestries tumbled like waterfalls down the side walls; a great purple banner splashed magnificently across the width of the balcony. The centre of the banner held a coloured photograph of himself, underneath it the simple inscription: *Love Conquers All*. There were other slogans discreetly inserted into the vast surface of the hall: *Love Thy Neighbour as Thyself, Love is Perfection, Live a Life of Love, The World Needs Love*.

Christian knew them all by heart, had composed many of them himself, but they no longer had any individuality for him. Rather were they a part of the familiar pattern, fitting neatly among the streams of colour, of scarlet and white and purple – the whole interweaving and merging into a bright, harmonious background. It was always the same background, no matter the size or shape of the hall; this was one of the items faithfully attended to by one of his zealous, efficient secretaries. Sometimes, after a long uncomfortable railway journey, perhaps a descent into the strange bleak environment of some provincial town, he was glad to be able to find himself in an atmosphere so warmly familiar. But there were other times when he resented the sameness of it, when he longed to see a different set of colours, a different shape to the hall – even if it became ungainly and unattractive.

'And now I have pleasure in introducing –' the chairman began pronouncing, a surge of importance colouring his voice. Hearing the familiar cue, Christian emerged from the shadows and began walking towards the raised dais at the front of the platform. An initial, spontaneous burst of applause welcomed him.

Before him a vast sea of white, upturned faces swayed backwards and forwards, as if according to some strange rhythmic ritual – a sea that stretched far away until it became lost, like any sea, into a misty horizon. As he looked, fascinated, the applause trickled away and he suddenly felt the familiar reverent hush, always frightening to him in its swiftness and intensity. It swept across the hall, drowning the desultory flow of coughings and whisperings, silencing the fidgety movements. Decisively, one by one, the huge arc lamps dimmed and went out. Then, a single bright spotlight stabbed across the hall like a warning, pointing finger. It flooded the small wooden dais in a precise circle of brightness. It cast a shimmering glow about the thin, angular hand-rails, poured harsh sunshine upon the sheaves of yellow daffodils that spurted up around the foot of the dais. There was no avoiding the implication, no ignoring the automatic command. He walked up the three small steps on to the dais and took his place squarely in the centre of the spotlight: fitting, neatly, the final piece, into the pattern.

For a moment he stood there, letting the merciless light reveal him, the external him, to the expectant audience – letting them see, so they could marvel at, his delicate beauty, the slight, ethereal glow of other-worldness that surrounded his whole being. He held his fine, smooth head at a certain angle, an angle at which – so his advisers had decided – the spotlight accentuated the impressive high dome of his forehead and threw a pleasant gleam across the dark glossy hair falling back across his head. At that angle, too, the light slanted across his face and emphasised the lines of the noble features, imparting tiny graceful shadows that gently cloaked the extreme softness and youthfulness, giving him a wiser and more mature appearance.

Christian stood there now, his thin body in its simple black robe swaying ever so slightly, like a leaf in the wind, his long well-kept fingers caressing the gleaming handrail, his eyes half-closed as if in meditation: waiting, as he always had to wait, for the flow of words that would eventually come pouring out. As he waited, he wondered, a trifle wistfully, what they were thinking out there, what was going on behind each white shadowy mask, that hid a world so remote. He thought of them coming to the hall, crowding into buses, standing in train corridors, the fortunate few sitting back in their taxis or their motor-cars, all of them hurrying, pressing on, afraid of missing anything. He saw them leaving their faraway homes, their three-roomed flats and their crumbling tenements and their bright ugly suburban villas and their austere Georgian houses, and their remote country mansions; hurrying away from their half-finished housework, from their typewriters and their files, their shops and their factories; gulping down a meal somewhere, diving on into the blackness, winding their way through the shadowy streets, suddenly plunging out of the dark into the brightness of the hall, into a fantastic new world of aisles and tapestries, scarlet sashes, white robes; Mark Christian.

How many, he wondered, had come before, and how many were experiencing for the first time the vast hall, the awed crowd, the spotlighted figure, the air of tense expectancy. And what about afterwards, when they went away in their ones and their twos and their threes, the fat ones and the thin ones, the old ones and the young ones: the crying ones and the sneering ones, round-eyed ones and the blank-eyed ones, would they go away as they came, unsatisfied, querulous, uncertain ...? He tried to visualise them afterwards, but they had disappeared into the darkness and were lost, he clutched at shadows only ... he could not, somehow, insert himself across the great void between them, and into their bright, warm, unknown lives ...

He tried again, forced himself to recapture memories of the

ones who came surging round at the end of the meetings, the ones with faces suddenly lit up and eyes shining, even full of tears and the ones wanting to say something and unable to say it. Ah, yes, there were those, they were reality, they were humanity, poor suffering humanity. To them he brought a message, to them his words meant something ... They were there now, out in the vast dark world – he began, excitedly, to add colour to their white anonymity – Oh, who were they and what were they thinking out there across the sea?

Now they were looking up, looking at him, pleading, beseeching ... Their eyes became steely magnets, pulling at him, dragging things out of him, tugging at his mind, his heart, his soul, his whole being. Gladly, spontaneously, he gave himself up, throwing out his arms in their triumphant gesture.

'Oh, my brothers,' he cried, his eyes shining, 'Oh, my brothers and sisters!' – and the way he said it made it sound like a great trumpet blast, filling the huge hall and echoing far round the world.

He did not talk from memory or from manuscript, he talked from the heart. Suddenly, abruptly, it was as if a secret spring had been tapped. The words came pouring out from the very depths of him – but they were so beautiful, so exquisitely fashioned that they might have been created by another person for all he knew about them: perhaps were. That was the wonder of it, the great insurmountable fact that made him go on and on, leaving him no choice, no right to doubt, no right to rest, no right to attempt his escape from the demands of the tremendous edifice that had grown up around him.

For what he said was wisdom: that the whole world recognised. Captured by the patient reporters and observers who followed him about, the words became flaming apostles. They were repeated, made into messages, into sermons, into lessons, they took visible shape in newspapers, in pamphlets, in books, they resounded over the ether, they reached the furthest corners of the earth. Wherever there were men and women with questing minds, there, eventually, would the message of Mark Christian be received. It was a message that might temporarily be drowned by the blarings of politicians and war lords, but it was a message that would live longer than any of theirs, for, as Christian would cry out: 'Only Love Can Save the World.' That was why every hall had its sea of faces, its hushed, expectant, hopeful silence, that was why he could never cease, not when there was so much evil, pain and suffering, so much calvary, and so little happiness in the world.

Tonight, as always, he brought them the message of Love, calling out, in his strange, vibrant voice to the bus drivers and the housewives and the bank clerks and the shop assistants, the soldiers and the sailors, the princes and the paupers, pleading with them to love the whole world as they would love their mothers, their brothers, their wives, their children.

'We need love, pure love now as never before, love instead of hate, love instead of resentment, love that can break down all barriers, make wars impossible, bring peace to us all ... Love between fellow-men, love and warm companionship and friendship, love in the home, embracing everyone, sweeping away the loneliness and the emptiness. Open your hearts to those around you, do not shut them out!'

Evenly, persuasively, he let the words flow on, hardly moving as he spoke, only sliding his hands backwards and forwards along the frail hand-rail. It did not really matter what he said if only he could bridge the gap, to make contact with some of them.

'If only you will let love enter your hearts and let it flourish there, oh, what a vast change you will see in your lives!' he declared to them, and, listening in reverent silence, they envied this man alight with the love of humanity. 'Love will bring an end to your emptiness and your loneliness, it will bring new life to you!' he told them impressively, and their eyes lit up with the warm, wistful hope that he gave them. He leant far forward across the dais, his arms outstretched as if trying to bring their endless, childlike humanity into his eager loving embrace. 'Oh, believe me,' he cried, 'Love can be a part of you, like the colour of your skin, the sound of your voice, and then you love each one and everyone!' And many thousands of eyes looked covetingly upon this gifted one who had achieved such harmony, such true love and happiness.

He went on, pouring himself out to them creating for them, by his vivid gestures, his compelling words, the very reality of love. He told them simple little parables illustrating the fellowship of love. His voice took on a glow of passionate conviction as he talked of the joys of friendship and fellowship, of the way in which love could bring warmth into a life, into a home, into a community. He talked faster and faster, seeming to become possessed by what he was saying, so that he became something more than a human being, and more like a living flame, that spread out to every corner of the hall, lighting up the hearts and faces of the listeners. They began giving themselves up to his pleading, persuasive voice, letting the truth of his message enter into them.

It was then, perhaps, that he achieved his miraculous, fleeting sense of fusion with all their distant anonymity; but always, even as he attained this peak, so he became suddenly exhausted and drained of everything, of the breath and energy to go on speaking. The last few words came out slowly and stiffly, bringing with them, as they died away, a queer dissatisfaction; and then a feeling of being frightened now that the moment had gone, was too late to be recaptured, and there remained only the familiar pattern.

But when he finished speaking his face was still lit up, his eyes bright, and there was no doubt about the wild wave of clapping and cheering that suddenly burst through the silence. When, suddenly weary, he made to move, they began crying out his name, chanting it like they were chanting the name of a god, until he came down from the dais and went to the edge of the platform. He was too tired to speak, and they did not want him to speak, they only wanted him to stand there for them to worship. He saw the sea suddenly rise up high and then pour towards him, and they came surging around the platform, they with their thousands of unknown faces.

He held his hands out to them like a father to his children but he saw, behind his smile, that they instinctively flinched, drawing back nervously as the slaves from the master. He dropped his hands and stood smiling down at them, trying to give himself and his love to them. One or two touched his feet, gazed up at him. He looked into their eyes, pinpoints of mystery, and smiled: 'Have no fear.'

Strange cloaks of fright slid over their eyes, he felt them recede into awe and reverence. He had the extraordinary certainty that if he moved down to them the tide would turn, the sea begin to fall back. He was too tired to attempt to test them, all he could do was to stand there and try and feel himself a part of them. For the moment, lost on the triumphant wave of his eloquence, he had felt himself surge to meet them, entering their hearts. Now he saw, even as their unhappy faces were floating around his feet, a steel insurmountable barrier between them.

At last he turned and began walking slowly back across the platform, still surrounded by the steady flow of their gratitude. As he went the spotlight followed him, throwing his slight figure into solitary relief, casting a thin, lengthening shadow across the floor. Coming among the people on the platform, local dignitaries, churchmen, schoolteachers, women's leaders he saw that they, too, were clapping, they, too, had their faces lit up, as if with a new light of love. Ah! ... He stopped and smiled at them, making an involuntary movement towards them. They called out: 'Thank you, thank you!' – 'A beautiful speech' – 'You have brought us the truth, Mr Christian!'

But when he bent forward towards them they seemed somehow to retire before him, when he stretched out a hand to grasp the nearest one, the woman drew back as if in awe and slowly bowed down before him. His hand remained outstretched, in mid-air; watching it he thought how foolish and empty it looked, and he turned and half-walked, half-ran the remaining distance to the tiny door at the back of the platform.

Afterwards, in the little ante-chamber, the chairman came and introduced his wife and his daughter and some friends, and their friends. He shook hands warmly with them and thought it must be his imagination that their hands seemed to be stiff and cold, to slip awkwardly out of his grasp. Christian said, sincerely: 'I am very glad to meet you.' The chairman was rosy-cheeked and tubby, a friendly man, earnest but good-humoured about it, a family man with an affectionate twinkle in his eyes. He had made a short but moving speech of introduction, speaking in a slow gruff voice. But now he flushed and looked ill-at-ease, mumbling conventional words and shifting from leg to leg. His wife and daughter, austerely dressed for the occasion, smiled politely but hardly spoke.

Christian tried desperately to insert himself into their lives. He wondered if they were going to invite him to their house. Perhaps sitting cosily together, in the friendly firelight, the strange barriers that surrounded him would break down. He let his mind run ahead, half in hope yet not without something approaching dread: times before it had happened, and the barriers had remained, looming higher than ever in the small, tense atmosphere of privacy. Perhaps, he thought ... but even then they were bowing low before him, and for half-an-hour they glided around him like they would before an idol, or a mystic god or (he could not help thinking) an animal at the zoo.

His secretaries, two mild serious-eyed young students, edged unobtrusively towards him, bringing him a cup of tea, and a sandwich. He looked at them gratefully: they worked so hard, so untiringly; he owed them much. He felt a sudden warmth towards them at the thought of someone sharing, in part at least, his life ... He raised a hand in greeting, thinking of something to express what he felt.

They nodded gravely, then one of them said, cutting across his half-formed sentences: 'You must not overtire yourself, you must go home and have a good night's rest ... Tomorrow you are to speak at a women's conference in the morning, then you are a guest of honour at a Rotary Club luncheon, in the afternoon there is a visit to a children's home; and then we must catch the express up North – it will be a big meeting, there will be many thousands waiting to hear your message.'

The other broke in smoothly, re-assuringly: 'But do not

worry, we will make all arrangements, none of these material things will be allowed to disturb your mental repose.' They lowered their heads deferentially, were about to slide into the background again –

'Please,' he said awkwardly, 'Thank you so much for what you have done – you are not going now?' In his mind floated the intangible shadows of what he wanted to say, something about going out together, perhaps for a meal; or walking home together, planning a holiday, away from everything.

But they were only smiling patiently, regretfully, at him. And now beckoning:

'You must rest ... See, we have a car arranged, it is waiting for you outside as soon as you can leave. Will you come?'

'Yes,' he said resignedly, and let them guide him quietly away from the room, leaving the chairman and the churchmen and their wives to vanish forever into their shadowy domestic worlds.

But after the taxi had gone a little way he made the driver stop and paid him off. Then, hunching up his shoulders and thrusting his hands deep into the pockets of his overcoat he walked along quiet pavements into a night hazy with drizzling rain. He walked aimlessly, wishing only to delay his final arrival. As he went he began to notice vague echoes of night – the sound of a late bus, its wheels hissing over the wetness, the pitter-patter of a stranger's footsteps, coming louder and then fading away. Occasionally a shadow loomed up and slid past him, a vague figure, head bent down against the rain, hurrying to some unimaginable home. Sometimes he stopped and watched the shadow disappearing, fascinated by the thought of a human being, a whole life, coming within a hair's-breadth of fusing with his own, so near and yet so far apart. Fascinated, too, to think that perhaps the shadow was one of millions who had at some time listened enraptured to Mark Christian, who had perhaps even bowed before him, whose whole life had perhaps been changed by words of his, by the impact of his message of love ... Oh, it was hard not to know, to be lost in the dark among so many shadows. If only some of the shadows could somehow materialise into something alive and definite ... he began to play, dreamily, with the thought ... if only one shadow ... Perhaps this shadow, this shadow, fleeting by like a wraith in the mist, this very shadow?

A shape loomed out of the darkness, passed close by him, receded again. Forlornly, almost with a sense of detachment, he walked quickly in pursuit, not thinking at all, just letting himself drift on the wave of his impulse. Down one street and across another, then out along the grey, cold pavements. The footsteps ahead of him moved quickly and sharply; his own crept after it in short uneasy jerks, almost as if they were not his own. He could see no more than a bobbing head, a shadowy movement in the night, a sigh of breath, a click of sharp heels, a whole world walking away from him, walking away from him, walking away from him ... And needing him, Oh Lord, perhaps needing him, wanting him, perhaps, unknowingly, searching for him, calling out for him? 'Christian! Christian! Christian!' – the cry swirling up from the very dark depths of the sleeping river.

He ran forward urgently, holding his hands forward in the darkness, towards the sound of the footsteps, towards echoes that suddenly died. In a moment he had reached the shadow, pausing under the silver light of a street-lamp.

'I – ' he said. 'I – thought – I –'

But there were no more words, they remained buried, too deep, forgotten, unborn. Looking by the faint unreal light, he saw a girl, any girl: the body hidden in the darkness, the face turned up to the light so that little shadows fell around the eyes and curved sadly around the drooping mouth. The face was a garish mask of whiteness, without expression, without meaning; but the eyes were unmasked, the eyes, even as they smiled their bright false smile, held in their shining depths age-old glimpses of suffering, of resentment of accusation. The eyes asked a terrible question, tendered a frightening invitation.

Christian turned blindly and ran, ran away and away through the dark streets, until he was almost choking for breath. His eyes remained half-closed; some sort of instinct somehow guided him through the maze, brought him at last to the quiet shuttered hotel.

A night porter laboriously unbolted the door and let him in, guiding him through a darkened hallway and into the empty lounge. He looked at Christian respectfully and asked if he would like anything to drink. 'No, thank you,' said Christian, and he walked swiftly out of the friendless lounge and up the stairs to his room on the first floor. He hesitated momentarily, his hand on the door, then went in. He found the curtains securely drawn and a neat electric fire burning, remembered with fleeting gratitude the cheerful maid who had fussed around him – now asleep and dreaming in her own world.

He shut the door after him, hung up his coat and walked across to the fire, standing against the mantelpiece. Without the light on the room had a cosy appearance. Standing where he was he was reminded familiarly of standing in one of the vast halls, the cynosure of all eyes, preparing to pour out his message to the thousands of human souls waiting eagerly in the misty shadows. He almost fancied he could hear them murmuring, clapping, cheering – yes, it was easy to imagine ... He thought, in sudden hope, of them there in the room, their faces raised, just human beings like himself. People, people, people – could he not open their hearts and release their love? Would there not be an end to all the world's emptiness and loneliness and lovelessness? Was it not his task, was he not their saviour, bringing them redemption, new hope, a new life? He could see their shadows outlined by the firelight against the opposite wall. They were standing up, holding out their arms towards him, coming to him for love, for happiness. They were bringing their own warm, human love, to him – to him, to him. 'Oh, my brothers! Oh, my brothers!'

Then with a swift, savage movement, he leaped across to the electric light switch and flooded the room, pouring bright electric sunshine upon his world: the Chippendale arm-chair, the polished writing-desk, the pilot reading-lamp by the bed – the smooth, blue, anonymous bedcover. For moments of eternity he stared remorselessly at every smooth curve and precise corner of lifelessness, and all around him there was a great silence, broken only by the steady ticking of a clock – each tick the measure of his frustration, his loneliness and his failure.

XVII

Library Service

This is a true story, that's what makes it all the more remarkable. I mean, it's not exactly what you expect when you amble along on that weekly visit to the local library, is it?

We're lucky; our local library is only a few minutes' walk, and to tell the truth I go there more than once a week. I like to sit in the reference room and thumb through the periodicals – my word, couldn't possibly afford to buy them these days, could you?

Well, what happened is this. After a spell in the reference room as usual I went down and browsed around the library shelves. Myself, I usually settle for a couple of good novels and one nice solid bit of non-fiction – something to get my teeth into, so to speak. You know the sort of thing, books of adventure, travel, sea voyages and so on.

It was that kind of book I picked up on this occasion. I can't remember the title exactly but it was all about a group of lively young English lads who'd bought an old Land Rover and set off to drive half way across the world. A really gripping tale it was, and I was quite sorry to have to put it down to watch the news on telly at the usual time. I was living on my own then, a little bachelor flat I suppose you'd call it, and glad of the telly for company – just shows, doesn't it, how already I must have been getting into the set ways of a bachelor?

Well, after the news I picked up the book, opened it where I'd folded back the corner of the page, and started reading again. I turned a couple of pages or so and then – well, there it was – the photograph. No, I don't mean an illustration in the book or anything like that – but a separate photograph, an ordinary black and white snapshot.

Er, well, ordinary isn't quite the right word. Ordinary in shape and type, yes, but not at all in content. It was in fact a photograph of a girl, a very pretty girl – no, no, I must make it clear, a really beautiful girl. I don't know where it had been taken but it must have been either at sea, or beside the sea, because all you could see in the background was a vast horizon of sky and water. There were several clouds scattered about the sky and the sea looked pretty disturbed, too. But it was closer at hand that really caught your attention. This girl's face, half turned back to look at the camera, smiling, mischievous, alive – oh, yes, quite beautiful.

I don't mind telling you that picture really floored me. Within a moment I had lost all interest in those poor lads and their Land Rover, which had just about got stranded somewhere in the middle of a desert – as far as I was concerned, from then on they could be stranded there till this day. I had eyes only for the photograph.

I can remember how I took it from between the pages of the book and held it up to examine it more clearly, looking on the back to see if maybe there might be a name and address, or at least that of the shop where it had been printed. But no, not a word, just virgin white, blank and anonymous.

I couldn't leave things at that, of course. I just had to try and find out something about the girl. You wouldn't think it an impossible task, would you, really? I mean – how would *you* go about things? Yes, that's right, just what I did. The next day I went along to the library and stood there clearing my throat once or twice and trying to catch the attention of the slightly forbidding young lady who somehow always seemed to be on duty whenever I came in. At last she came over, wearing her usual slight frown – a pity, I always felt, because really she wasn't a bad-looking girl. I supposed it was all that reading she had to do, made her screw up her eyes perhaps. More than once I'd been tempted to make the suggestion: 'Do you think you need glasses, miss?' But I felt a bit shy about that, none of my business really.

Funnily enough I didn't feel a bit shy about asking her about the photograph. I just pulled it out of my pocket and showed it to her and explained the circumstances:

'Of course, I suppose strictly speaking it's library property, ha-ha! To tell you the truth I'm more than a little intrigued. Someone must have accidentally left the photo in the book and – well, I must say I'd really like to meet that girl.'

The library girl gave me quite a strange look then. Hard to say exactly what it was, really. Resentment? Annoyance? Pique – yes, maybe that was it, pique.

'I'm sure *I've* no idea,' she said brusquely. 'How do you expect me to be able to help? I deal with hundreds of books every day.'

'Yes, I do realise that. But I just wondered if maybe – well, you could look up the address of the last borrower? That would be a great help.'

The library girl pursed her lips. I was afraid she was going to refuse to help. She certainly shook her head at me reprovingly.

'Really, you are being a bit of a nuisance. Still ... all right, I'll have a look in the files.'

Come to think of it she was probably bending the rules a bit but anyway she gave me an address. It wasn't far from my home, so later that evening I went along and knocked at the door. I didn't know quite what I was expecting, whether the actual vision herself – no, I suppose I hadn't dared to imagine that far. But I certainly hoped to find out something.

Alas, the person who answered the door was a middle-aged woman, her grey hair in curlers. She looked puzzled when I explained what I had come about but agreed it was her who had had the book out – and a rattling good story it had been, too, she'd really enjoyed it.

I showed her the photograph hopefully. She took a look and shook her head decisively.

'Sorry, young fellow, but I've never seen that before. It certainly wasn't in the book when I had it out, or I'd have been sure to notice.'

Well, that was a disappointment, I must say. The next day I took my problem back to the library girl. She gave a shrug.

'Well, that's it, isn't it?'

I looked at her incredulously.

'What do you mean, that's it? Do you think I'm going to stop there?'

'Well ... you *are* a determined young man, aren't you?'

'Hey, come off it,' I felt bound to say. 'I'm probably no older than you are.'

The library girl paused to give this remark consideration. I noticed she was like that, given to weighing things up. But at least she wasn't afraid to take decisions, I'd grant her that.

'Well, we needn't start arguing about ages. Instead, let's put our heads together and consider this little problem of yours.'

She was as good as her word, too. As soon as her shift was ended she came over and joined me in the reference room where I was sheafing through the magazines in a desultory sort of way.

'Well, I've made a few inquiries, been showing your photo around.'

'And?'

She grimaced.

'I'm afraid no one recognises it.' She smiled suddenly – funny, I'd never seen her smile before, not really. On duty she always looked so severe. Now – well, it made her look quite different, that smile. Softer, nicer, warmer. At any other time I might have felt like telling her so – but of course now I had more important things on my mind.

'Well, what are we going to do then?'

I managed to introduce a note of accusation into my voice, hoping it would make her feel involved – after all I certainly needed her help, she was literally my only hope. I was relieved when she obviously accepted the challenge.

'To tell you the truth,' she said, and again that faint, rather heart-warming smile 'I've already got the whole library staff going on your problem.'

'You have?'

'Yes.' Her eyes began dancing a little, as if with hidden mischief. 'The fact is they're all terribly intrigued. I think they feel, well ...' She gave me another of those curious looks which I found difficult to define except that I sensed they were not unfavourable. 'It is all rather romantic, isn't it?'

'Yes, of course it's romantic,' I said, rather exasperatedly. 'That's why I'm going to all this trouble.'

'Mmmmh, of course.' The library girl nodded her head understandingly. As she did so her long dark hair fell forward in disarray so that she had to push it back, a rather charming gesture I couldn't help thinking. 'I do understand – for you it's become a kind of quest – a pilgrimage?'

I looked at her admiringly.

'You put it just right. How did you know?'

She smiled faintly.

'I do read books myself, you know, and quite often romantic ones.'

Her eyes suddenly sparkled. I warmed to her greatly.

'Look,' I said, unhappily. 'What's the chances? Do you think I've any hope of tracing her?'

I must have looked downcast or something because suddenly I felt the library girl's hand over mine, friendly and re-assuring. To tell you the truth, I was quite sorry when she removed it.

'Don't you worry,' she said firmly. 'I'll help all I can. What's more, you can feel sure the whole library staff are behind you, too.'

She was speaking the truth, too. Not only did she herself make endless inquiries, but it soon became apparent that wheels were turning within wheels – I even learned that the head librarian himself had been so intrigued that he had gone off with the famous photograph to head office.

'But what for?' I said puzzledly.

'Don't you see?' said the library girl. We were sitting having a cup of coffee in the little cafe opposite the library ... somehow we'd got in the habit over the past few days of making that our meeting place, reporting latest progress and so forth.

'Don't you see – it's very clever. He thinks the photograph might be of one of the library girls. You know, maybe someone who handled the book after that woman brought it back.'

I didn't look very impressed.

'Sounds unlikely to me.' I said rather grumpily.

And so it proved. No one in head office recognised the photograph.

Rosie told me so at our next meeting. Somehow her name didn't really surprise me. Before I'd got to know her it would have done – but not now.

'You know,' I said airily, over our coffees. 'You're just what I've always imagined a girl called Rosie would be like.'

'Oh, yes?' For a moment there was a shiver of that old severity.

'That reminds me,' I went on. 'When I used to come in the library – why did you always look at me in that funny sort of way?'

'What funny sort of way?'

'You know – like you nearly did just then.'

Rosie lifted her chin and pouted slightly.

'If you want to know I thought you seemed a rather arrogant fellow.'

'Did you?' I said, rather wonderingly. 'Really?'

'Yes, I did. Really.'

There was a brief pause then. I imagine we were both wondering whether to continue the argument – but somehow it seemed a little ridiculous. After all, we were now partners in an important enterprise.

'Tell you what,' said Rosie. 'I'll try and find out if it might have been one of the girls who *used* to work here.'

'But wouldn't you remember?'

'No, silly – I mean, before my time.'

It seemed to me a pretty hopeless idea, but Rosie went ahead with inquiring. And then off on one or two rather wild ideas. And time went by ... and we got nowhere.

And then – well, we were sitting one afternoon in the cafe staring idly out at the passing crowd – at least, Rosie was staring and I – well, for some reason I found myself staring not at the passing crowd, but at Rosie. I had never before noticed what classical sort of features she had – yes, when you *really* looked at Rosie, why she was very pretty, very pretty indeed. Almost, you might say, beautiful.

'Now about that photo,' Rosie began. 'It seems to me ...'

I remember that was the moment I took out the photograph and held it up in the air thoughtfully while I looked over it, into Rosie's deep dark eyes. My word, I couldn't see anything except those marvellous eyes.

'Oh, about that photograph,' I said huskily.

'Yes?'

Very deliberately I took the photograph between my fingers and tore it up into small white strips – and then, with rather magnificent aplomb I thought, dropped them into an empty coffee cup.

Rosie stared at me in astonishment.

'Why did you do that?'

I grinned back.

'I suppose to put it rather crudely because a real live library girl at hand is worth a dozen silly old photos in a book.'

'Well – thanks very much!'

Rosie pouted. When she pouted she looked absolutely delicious. I couldn't resist it: I leaned over the table and kissed her, very firmly. She was very kissable; much more kissable than any photograph.

And – well, that's how it all happened. A true story, as I say. I still go along to my local library quite regularly, but now I've got an extra reason. You see, my wife works there.

XVIII

Married Bliss

People were surprised when the Millingtons broke up. Somehow they were a couple one had come to – well, take for granted, I suppose. They were very much what is generally termed a well-suited pair, I don't think there can be much doubt about that. You know how it is, sometimes you see a couple walking down a street and you simply can't help thinking – why, they look as if they were just made for each other. That was just the sort of reaction people had to the Millingtons: to Clara with her blaze of reddish hair and her strong, finely-based features and her sensual way of walking so that even though she was no more than five feet or so men always turned to give an admiring stare – and to Richard, too, tall and dark, rather thin but graced by a kind of haggard handsomeness, and with gentle brown eyes that promised sympathy. Oh, yes, they were a very complementary pair.

They'd been together a long time, too. That's important, really. People grow together, even sometimes against their wishes, if they live together, spend all their time together. Something about the daily routine shared, moments in common, it all helps to breed a kind of mutual sympathy – or, the more cynical might say, binds the web tighter. Joking apart, togetherness suited the Millingtons. They actually seemed to blend together in a kind of instinctive harmony, to form a structure of their own. Indeed though at first you might be conscious of meeting Clara, or perhaps Richard, distinctly drawn to one vivacious personality or perhaps instead to the rather more austere one – in the end it was as if the two merged into a single unit and you found yourself thinking of 'Clara and Richard', or more simply, 'the Millingtons'. That's how you would write the invitations if you were planning a dinner or throwing a party – 'the Millingtons'. And usually you would be glad of their bright company, for somehow they brought with them an air of happy accord, of good cheer, even of a sort of beauty. They were, as I say, a handsome couple. But, above all, in these uncertain times I think for us all they represented a kind of security: 'the Millingtons', firm and fixed, a sort of long-term investment in marital harmony.

Of course, circumstances could be said to have encouraged their togetherness for they were one of those husband and wife teams at work as well as at home. They ran a fashionable antique shop much frequented by families in the area, and so not only would you find them together in the evenings, but in the daytime, too. Sometimes they would be together in the shop, Richard working at a large desk on the accounts, Clara floating around with a duster in her hand – other times they would be at one of the local auction sales, Richard quiet and thoughtful with a shrewd eye upon a bargain, Clara with her face animated with a child-like excitement. It was quite extraordinary, really how much of a unit they seemed.

Yet they were a family, too. That added to their reassuring air of permanence – three children, all girls, all imprinted with the charm of their parents. Three pretty teenage girls forming just the right sort of family background ... Small wonder, really, that in our town the phrase 'the Millingtons' had come to be synonymous with a kind of holy veneration for 'the family', 'conjugal bliss' and so on.

Which made it all the more of a shock, as I say, when the news got around. Shock is hardly a strong enough word really – catastrophe conveys more of the feeling. You see we had come to look on the Millingtons as a kind of institution. They were simply part of the stable and familiar structure of our lives. Suddenly, faced with the abrupt disappearance of this sense of security we were – well, frightened, I suppose.

Our first reaction was to try and pretend nothing of the sort had really happened. 'Clare and Richard? Separated? Absolute nonsense. Never known such a happy couple. Just rumours ...'

Then, when Richard moved out to live in a hotel and it became clear that for once rumour was only too well-founded, alas, we felt it was time for some more positive action. When one of the foundations of everyday life is threatened, something must be done. We held a few hurried meetings and I was sent off to interview Richard in his unfamiliar new surroundings of an anonymous hotel bedroom.

It wasn't a very productive interview. I found Richard reclining in a comfortable armchair with his feet up and a bottle of whisky to hand. As soon as he saw me he shook his head vehemently.

'It's no good. I can guess what you've come about.'

'But – Clara?'

'Clara's well able to take care of herself. You know that. She's a businesswoman. She won't starve. And anyway I'm making her an allowance.'

'Well, then, what about the children?'

'Oh, go on with you. I've been thinking about the children for more than twenty years. Now they can fend for themselves, it won't do them any harm. Besides, Laura's getting married, Julia's at university and Helen has gone to live with a friend in London. So what's bothering you?'

I retired after another twenty minutes of unsuccessful pleading, to report back glumly that my particular mission had been a failure.

'I can't understand – he actually sounded like he was quite *glad* to be on his own.'

We weren't giving up easily, however. My next call was upon Clara, still installed in her large family house up the road.

Frankly I expected to find Clara rather low in spirits. After all, twenty-two years of marriage tossed aside, broken asunder, couldn't be much of a joke. My first instinct on

seeing her was to search her face for signs of secret sorrow – no
doubt, I thought, she's been crying. But I must admit she did
not look particularly sad; indeed she seemed to be positively
blooming – I had hardly ever seen her looking so attractive.

'Clara – look, I'm terribly sorry about – I mean, we've only
just heard about you and Richard. It's most upsetting, really
terrible.'

'Oh, that!' With a toss of her head Clara appeared to
dispose of the subject. 'Oh, I expect he'll survive.'

'But I mean – well, you and he – the family – ?'

Somewhat to my irritation Clara proceeded to explain as
succinctly as her husband had done just how well the family
could manage on its own.

'But that's not the point,' I burst out at last, in some
annoyance. 'It's – it's not right, your separating like this. I
mean – well, you and Richard, you've always been as devoted
to one another. I mean to say – why?'

Clara lit a cigarette and smiled coolly.

'Oh, he hasn't gone off with another woman or anything
like that.'

'I appreciate that – I've seen him sitting all lonely in a
miserable hotel bedroom.'

'Lonely?' Clara's eyebrows raised slightly. 'Did he say he
was lonely?'

'Well, er, not exactly …'

'Quite.' Suddenly she took a deep breath and held her hand
out in an explanatory gesture. 'Don't you understand? For
twenty-two years Richard and I have lived in each other's
pockets. We've hardly ever been apart. Why, we've been like –
like – '

'Like a shining example of a really happy marriage,' I said
stubbornly.

'Exactly.' Clara blew a cloud of smoke into my eyes. 'And I
can tell you it's been a terrible strain. In fact, I just don't know
how I've been able to stand it. Indeed I couldn't have done it if
it hadn't been for –' She gave a queer smile, 'If it hadn't been
for Richard. You see, he's always understood; why, he felt just
the same as me. Never mind, old dear, he used to say, just

hang on until the children are old enough – then we can be free.'

'Free?' I said blankly.

'Yes.' Clara suddenly got to her feet and whirled round, like a young girl. 'Free – free to enjoy life without any responsibilities at all. Oh, isn't it wonderful? Can't you imagine how I feel? Why, it's just like escaping from some sort of prison.'

'Well, really ...'

Of course, she had to be joking. Well, no, I could see she wasn't really. Well, then, probably she's been overworking, something like that. There must be some *reasonable* explanation.

But, it appeared, there wasn't. We all found it quite worrying when we sat around and discussed the situation. Time was passing, life was going on. Richard had been seen going about his affairs quite cheerfully and without a broken heart – he ran the antique shop on his own now. Clara for her part appeared to be indulging in a round of special visits to London. She had apparently even held a party – without Richard.

It really was too bad. We held conferences, we aired our views, we even on one occasion took a vote about our best possible course of action – but it all seemed to matter very little. Clara and Richard had definitely parted company and gone their own ways, and one of the pillars of our social life had crumbled. Clara was living her life, Richard his, it could only be a matter of time before they got involved with other people. Oh, it was a sad story ...

And then one day a strange thing happened. I didn't see it myself but one of the good ladies of the town did, with her own eyes, and she came rushing round to tell us.

'Guess what? I was travelling up to town the other day and who should be on the train sitting side by side but Clara and Richard. Yes, really.' A beaming smile. '*Together*!'

Could this be true? Was it just wish-fulfilment? At once we deployed our spies and soon – ah, soon the joyful reports began to come in. Richard and Clara seen walking across the common – Richard and Clara seen at the local cinema – Richard and Clara spied at a local sale together. Richard and Clara, Richard and Clara … Yes, there could be no doubt about it … and the supreme touch came, I felt, when at last at one of our regular social gatherings, there they were, together, Richard and Clara.

I lost no opportunity to draw Clara aside for a word of congratulations.

'I'm so happy for you both, my dear.'

Clara looked puzzled.

'But I thought you knew – we're separated.'

'Yes, yes – but not now. You've been seen together so often.'

'But of course.' Clara smiled sweetly and held her hands out. 'And so nice it's been. Do you know I was married to Richard for twenty-two years and this is the first time I've really *enjoyed* being with him.'

She looked at me caustically. 'Don't you believe me?'

I said I didn't. Clara laughed.

'Wait till you've been married twenty-two years. Just you wait!'

With that our conversation ended. Clara returned to the party and a moment later I saw her sharing drinks with Richard. They looked such a natural couple together the sight quite irritated me. When they were at last preparing to go I accosted Richard in the entrance hall.

'So you're going on with this – this charade?'

He swung his raincoat casually over his shoulder and gave me a wink. I must say he looked younger and more attractive than ever.

'Of course. Didn't I tell you how wonderful it is to be free again?'

'But you're with Clara!'

He looked round and saw his wife coming across the hall and made a mock gallant bow before she took his arm and they began walking away.

'Ah, but you see,' called out Richard over his shoulder. 'Now I have the freedom to choose. That makes all the difference.'

I think they were both laughing as they went off down the street. I have a pretty shrewd idea whom they were laughing at, too. They were laughing at me and all the other busybodies of the neighbourhood who had been trying to lead their lives for them. And, you know, I've a nasty feeling they might be right. Somehow 'the Millingtons' strike me as – well, a very happy couple, a very happy couple indeed.

XIX

A Balloon For Christmas

The enormous balloon came floating down the main street at about four o'clock in the afternoon, bobbing over the anonymous heads of the bustling worrying crowd – up and down, up and down, up and down – a vast red and blue balloon, decorated with a huge white outline of Father Christmas and perched on the end of a long thin stick.

Attached to the stick was the aching hand of an earnest young man wearing a new grey macintosh. He might have been a clerk or a shop assistant or a minor civil servant or any other kind of young man on his way home from work ... except for the huge balloon.

After a while, waving his hand about dramatically in order to avoid poking the stick into people's eyes or the balloon through a shop window, the young man joined a bus queue. In this stood a phlegmatic cross-section of the city's citizens: short men and tall men, fat ladies and thin ladies, young cheeky office boys and old grumbly grandfathers – all pre-occupied and morose, all weighed down by the terrible cares of the world. Not one of them, as it happened, carried a balloon.

At first the young man tried to pretend it was an everyday event for him to be standing there holding a large red and blue balloon. He hummed a tune, he looked round airily, he peered about for sight of a bus.

Then, unnervingly, he encountered a pair of steely grey eyes on him with what he took to be an accusing look. In fact their owner was probably trying to remember the time of an appointment or maybe the recipe for an evening meal: but to the young man the look spelled out condemnation, and he rushed to defend himself.

'Pretty, isn't it? The balloon I mean. Rather a silly idea really, I suppose. I mean ... well, to tell you the truth I don't quite know how it happened. You see, Mary, that's my wife, she said we could do with a balloon or two for Christmas and then I was walking along and – well, there was this, hanging outside a shop. So I went in and bought it.'

The young man paused for breath and looked round rather defiantly.

'She's three, my little girl. Mad about balloons, too. You see I–'

Suddenly his words fell on emptiness. The bus had arrived, the queue poured aboard as if carried by some relentless conveyor belt.

'Hey!' cried the young man quite angrily, and he plunged into the melee, squashing his clothes but somehow managing to preserve the balloon up and over, past the severely critical gaze of the conductor, and on into the narrow heaving jungle of the lower deck.

'Phew!' exclaimed the young man, mopping his forehead. He was standing, of course, third in a row. Now as the bus started with a vicious jerk the whole row was thrown off balance. Despairingly the young man grabbed for a tubular pillar.

Free, the balloon floated away and along through the bus until it came to rest in the lap of a stout lady with a detached, aristocratic look. She continued to stare out of the window as if by so doing she would in some way preserve a private world in which there could not conceivably be a Christmas balloon upon *her* lap.

Discreetly, even timorously, the young man leaned over and took back his balloon.

But a moment later there came another lurch and again the young man had to grab for support. This time, after balancing miraculously for some moments on the round egg-head of an elderly gentleman, the balloon slid into the expectant waiting grasp of a talkative type.

Here, obviously, was a ready humorist. Gleefully he held up the balloon for all to see.

'Well, ladies and gentlemen, what have we here? A bargain if ever I saw one: Come along now, who'll buy my nice balloon? You, sir? Sold to the gentleman on my right over there.'

And with a deft pat he sent the great balloon sailing past the young man's outstretched hand and into the astonished grasp of a middle-aged clerk. With the balloon the wit must have passed over some of his own abundant liveliness, for no sober clerk in his right mind would then have leaned forward – as this one now did – and blown, yes, playfully blown, the balloon into the face of a pretty young typist.

'I say, really – my balloon!' protested the young man helplessly.

But perhaps the typist didn't hear him. Suffice to say she had a mischievous tilt to her lips and a bright gleam in her dark eyes: hardly surprising then that with a delicious pout she lifted up the balloon and – whoosh! – it went sailing right across the crowded bus.

Too late now for the young man to gesticulate and open his mouth. Nobody would have heard him for the rumble of sound that swept around. An elderly gent in the back sportingly gave the balloon a tap with his spectacles case: a deft office boy gave it a helping hand; and in no time the balloon was being smacked backwards and forwards, to the accompaniment of hilarious shouts.

'Now then, now then, what's going on?' demanded the conductor, coming forward and rattling his ticket box angrily. 'You can't carry on like this – what do you think this is, a playground?'

He moved imperiously down the bus, quailing the momentary riot with the authority of his uniform, his badge, his peaked cap – above all his rather inhibiting thick eyebrows.

'And what may *this* be?' said the conductor witheringly, retrieving the balloon from a humble company director who, a few seconds before, had been about to clout it for six in gay abandon.

Feeling himself suddenly the centre of an Incident, the young man shrivelled up.

'It's – it's mine,' he said in a stage whisper.

'Oh,' said the conductor sarcastically. 'It's yours, is it? Well, just you see that you look after it, understand? Balloons, indeed! I've a good mind to charge you full fare for it.'

Martinet-like he glared round the bus as if daring any rebellious spirit to declare itself.

'Come along now – fares *please*!'

Before the onslaught of authority, like a pack of small children, the passengers subsided into a guilty silence. And yet, as the conductor moved around, a subtle conspiracy of mirth emerged. The humorist looked over at the clerk and gave a broad wink ... the clerk smiled politely at the typist ... she smiled roguishly at someone else ... somehow you could almost feel the silent ripples of laughter spreading around.

At first, still standing, cringing away from the formidable figure of the conductor while at the same time holding his balloon well out of reach of a large hat pin fixed into the hair of a lady in the seat below, the young man did not notice the atmosphere.

Then slowly, as its warmth began to penetrate, he looked around with more confidence. Everywhere it seemed there were eyes waiting to catch his, smiles at the ready, friendly nods. When the conductor had finished and returned to his platform and there was more room to move the young man felt himself positively expanding with a glow of good fellowship.

At last he felt compelled to make some comment.

'Silly idea, I suppose you're thinking. But you know what kids are like. I can't help thinking she'll get a lot of fun this Christmas, eh?'

Nobody answered directly. But somehow there was an answer in the air, warm and cheery, a curious sense of companionship which quite touched the young man, so that he nearly missed his stop.

When he finally got out awkwardly, still clutching his balloon, and then set off rather unsteadily down the road it seemed as if the whole busload of people turned to watch him. Indeed they stared after him almost hungrily, as if they didn't want to lose him completely, as if they wanted somehow to savour his existence down to the very last drop.

And long after the conductor had pressed the button and the bus drove away – indeed right until they had all reached their holly and mistletoe-decorated homes and were sitting by their fires, remembering to their families: 'I must tell you what happened today on the bus, there was this young man with a big Christmas balloon' – they were surprised to find themselves curiously happy, for a time perhaps almost unworried by all the world's cares.

As for the young man, as he turned the key in the lock and opened the door and went into the delightful familiarity of his own home he felt elevated, distinguished, triumphant – victor, as it were, of some great campaign.

'Hullo, darling!' he called out to his wife. 'Well, I *remembered*!'

And as he entered he brandished high the bright red and blue balloon with the puffed-out white shape of Father Christmas.

And the little girl played happily with it ever afterwards.